Jo's arm was f[...]
bedpost...with [...]

She blinked her lash[...]
reclining casually on h[...]head propped up
by his hand, unrestrained and completely in control.

"Good morning, sweetheart," Dean said lazily. "I
figured turnabout is fair play...especially when it
comes to indulging in fantasies."

An unexpected thrill coursed through Jo, chasing
away her alarm and eliciting a sensual heat that
spread to her feminine nerve endings. "And what
fantasy is that?" she dared to ask.

He splayed his long fingers on the mattress in front
of him and grinned roguishly. "*Me* captor, *you*
prisoner, with a little bondage thrown in for good
measure."

"There's just one thing you're missing, *Master*."

Amusement flickered across his expression. "And
what's that?"

"A *submissive* female," she replied impudently.

Dean chuckled, a deep, rich sound that made
Jo's body warm with awareness. "Oh, I'm not
worried about your surrender," he said, a little too
confidently. "After all, I'm a great believer in the
power of persuasion...."

Dear Reader,

I've had a blast writing supersensual stories for Blaze, and
with *A Wicked Seduction*, I had the opportunity to try something
different...to write about a female bounty hunter who ends up
wickedly seduced by her captive! Jo Sommers thinks she's come
across every kind of felon——until she takes gorgeous Dean Colter
into custody and discovers he has a thing for bondage.... Get
ready for a generous dose of red-hot sexual tension and
overwhelming erotic pleasures.

I hope you enjoy Jo and Dean's sexy, sizzling story. And I
hope you keep a lookout for my future Blaze releases——check
my Web site at www.janelledenison.com for updates. As well,
I love to hear from my readers. You can write to me at: P.O. Box
1102, Rialto, CA 92377-1102 (send a SASE for goodies!) or at
janelle@janelledenison.com.

Enjoy the heat!

Janelle Denison

Books by Janelle Denison

HARLEQUIN BLAZE
12—HEAT WAVES

HARLEQUIN TEMPTATION
759—CHRISTMAS FANTASY
799—TEMPTED
811—SEDUCED
832—SEDUCTIVE FANTASY
844—WILD FANTASY

A WICKED SEDUCTION

Janelle Denison

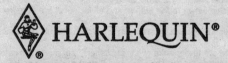

TORONTO • NEW YORK • LONDON
AMSTERDAM • PARIS • SYDNEY • HAMBURG
STOCKHOLM • ATHENS • TOKYO • MILAN • MADRID
PRAGUE • WARSAW • BUDAPEST • AUCKLAND

This book is dedicated to Laurie Pyke and Cheryl Shoemaker, two of the most devoted, enthusiastic fans a writer could ever hope for.

And to Don, for giving me the best fifteen years of my life. Happy anniversary.

ISBN 0-373-79037-6

A WICKED SEDUCTION

Copyright © 2002 by Janelle Denison.

1

FOR JOELLE SOMMERS, success was sweet and heady, and almost as exhilarating as great sex. Not that she'd had any of the latter lately, she thought wryly as she settled into her cushy office chair and propped her booted feet on the corner of her cluttered desk. But today's triumph more than made up for not having a man in her life. Sex provided a fleeting buzz compared to the elation of finally solving a difficult abduction or missing persons case and reuniting the individuals involved.

A smile tugged the corner of her mouth. When she'd made *that* idle comparison to a girlfriend during an evening of dinner and drinks, her friend blithely responded that she obviously wasn't getting laid by the right man, because the blissful aftereffects of sexual gratification could last for days on end.

Imagine that, Jo mused with wonder, unable to ignore the tingling warmth infusing her veins. She reached for a file folder next to her blotter and she sighed. That's about all she did these days…*imagine,* because she'd discovered that fantasies were so much better than *her* reality. Finding and wanting any man, let alone the *right* man, had become a tiresome quest that no longer appealed to her.

Unfortunately, Jo could always count on the men she dated to balk at her working in a male-dominated field filled with dangerous scenarios. Ultimately, they didn't understand her drive and passion for locating missing people, especially abducted children. And when they discovered she was an ex-cop and moonlighted as a bounty hunter on occasion, most felt compelled and obligated to lecture her on the perils of a *woman* capturing wanted fugitives. And how could she do such a thing without male protection?

Oh, puh-leeze! She'd had enough of that overbearing attitude from her two older brothers. While Cole and Noah had learned over the years to tamp down the guardian tendencies they'd honed at a very early age, both still managed to interfere with cases they believed were too much for her to handle. It was a battle she constantly struggled to win.

She couldn't seem to escape the male stereotypes that dictated she belonged in a safer line of business, or married, barefoot and pregnant, so she sacrificed sex—good, bad, or indifferent—for the thrill of the chase her cases provided. A piteous substitute for carnal pleasures, she knew, but she didn't need the frustration and hassles that came with involvement with the opposite sex.

Nor had any man inspired enough lust or passion to make it worth the effort, Jo mused as she stamped CASE CLOSED in red ink across the front label of the file she'd finally solved. Now *that* was the kind of satisfaction that drove and excited her.

A brisk knock sounded on her open office door, followed by the entrance of Melodie Turner, Sommers Investigative Specialists' front-end secretary. "A delivery just came for you," she announced, flashing a grin that lit up a pretty face untouched by cosmetics. "And it has the makings of a celebration."

Jo swept her feet back to the floor and sat up in her chair, eyeing the cellophane-wrapped gift basket Melodie placed in the center of her desk. Withdrawing the enclosed card, Jo smiled as she read the note from the Faron family thanking her for spending the past six months searching for, and for finding, their runaway daughter, Rachel.

It hadn't been an easy case. The thirteen-year-old girl had left a cold, difficult trail to follow by changing her name and appearance, but Jo had eventually tracked her down to a cult just outside of Sacramento, where Rachel had been selling beaded necklaces on the street. Convincing the teenager to return home had been much simpler than tracking her. The young girl, regretting her rash actions and no longer feeling defiant and rebellious, admitted to being homesick and missing her family. A perfect ending with a joyful reunion.

Unfortunately, not all of her missing person cases ended that way, and each one that did *was* a cause for celebration.

Jo peeled away the cellophane to reveal the treats hidden within the basket. "Umm, champagne and chocolate-covered strawberries. Care to join me in a toast?''

Melodie looked just as eager to sample the enticing delicacies. ''You don't have to ask me twice. It's ten after five, I'm technically off the clock, and I certainly don't have a better offer waiting for me.''

Jo slanted her an amused look. ''What, no hot Friday night date?''

Melodie rolled her eyes as she lifted the bottle of champagne from the basket, along with two plastic glasses. ''I haven't had a date, hot or otherwise, in months.''

Yeah, you and me both, sister. ''Maybe that's because you spend way too much time here at the office.'' Standing, Jo shrugged out of her jean jacket and hung it on the coat tree behind her desk. ''This is the first time in weeks that you've stopped working at five. And from what Noah has said, you've been staying as late as Cole in the evenings.''

Retrieving the bowl of big, plump chocolate-covered strawberries, Melodie shrugged and looked away, but Jo didn't miss the light shade of pink that swept across her cheeks. ''It's not like I have anything more exciting to occupy my nights, or a line of men beating down my door.''

''Well, you certainly aren't going to attract any male attention spending all your waking hours *here*.'' Jo's voice trailed off as she put two and two together. It seemed Melodie had a thing for Cole, and her boss had no clue she existed other than in her capacity as his dependable, reliable, devoted secretary.

Oh, man. Melodie had been working for Cole long enough, two years to be exact, to know that his interest in women ran toward the occasional undemanding fling—no promises involved—usually with sophisticated, leggy blondes who played by the same rules he did. Unfortunately, Melodie was the epitome of a respectable, decorous female in her plain, conservative outfits, and possessed the kind of good-girl tendencies and traditional values Cole avoided. If those qualities weren't enough to inspire Cole to keep his distance, Melodie was also the daughter of the man who'd become Cole's mentor after their own father had been shot and killed in the line of police duty. Cole had hired her as a favor to Richard Turner and had come to rely on Melodie as all bosses relied on their secretaries, but the odds of him noticing her as a woman were stacked heavily against her.

And Jo didn't have the heart to dash her friend's hopes.

While Melodie popped the plastic cork from the champagne bottle and poured the bubbly liquid into each of their glasses, Jo unbuckled her shoulder holster. Her brother insisted she wear a gun if she worked for him, but Jo knew it would take the direst of circumstances for her to actually *use* the weapon. She'd learned during her police academy training that you didn't retrieve your gun unless you were prepared to fire. When actually faced with that reality, she hadn't been able to pull the trigger. She still felt a painful twist in her heart thinking of the devastating results—

the death of her partner. She'd screwed up, and her failure had cost Brian Sheridan his life.

Since that fateful day over two years ago, Jo hadn't deluded herself with the belief that a gun would be her best source of defense. While she carried a weapon, she chose to protect herself with more controlled devices—a beanbag shotgun, a collapsible baton, and a black belt in martial arts. The combination served her well, and gave her a semblance of control over her actions.

Setting aside her holster, Jo picked up her drink and held it toward Melodie's. "Here's to another happy ending." Their plastic glasses clicked dully, and they each took a sip of the champagne. Then they indulged in the juicy, sweet strawberries dipped in a rich layer of chocolate, murmuring their appreciation for the delicious confection.

"Melodie?" a deep, rich voice abruptly called from the outer office.

At Cole's summons, Melodie popped up from her chair, abandoning her moment of relaxation. Jo nibbled on a piece of fruit and watched in amazement as the other woman circled her chair and was halfway to the door when Cole appeared, a file in hand. Melodie came to an abrupt stop before they collided and looked up at him with wide eyes.

"Did you need me?" Her voice was undeniably breathless.

Cole didn't notice, his demeanor strictly business. "Have you seen or heard from Noah?"

"He's been out of the office for the past two days

on surveillance for the Blythe divorce case,'' Melodie answered in her ever-efficient manner. ''He checked in this afternoon for messages, but said he probably wouldn't be back in the office until Monday.''

''Damn,'' Cole muttered beneath his breath, clearly annoyed at their brother's lack of availability. Though Noah worked for the company, he was definitely his own man and did things his own way. He was a drifter of sorts, an ex-Marine who worked when he needed the money, and played when his finances made it possible.

Cole dragged a hand along the back of his neck, as if the brusque movement could release the tension radiating from his body. ''By the way, did you get the final report and billing on the Cameron case typed up?''

''I put it on your desk about fifteen minutes ago. All it needs is your signature.''

He nodded succinctly, just as the office phone rang. Jo didn't bother reaching for the receiver on her desk, too interested in seeing how this scenario played out.

Another loud jingle.

Cole lifted a dark brow expectantly at Melodie as if to say, ''Aren't you going to get that?'' Too much a creature of habit, and too eager to please, Melodie automatically slipped around him and headed down the hall to answer the front-end phone.

Jo licked the sticky sweetness of candied strawberry from her fingers as her brother approached her desk. ''Jeez, Cole, would it kill you to answer the phone?'' When he gave her a blank look, she added drolly, "Melodie is off the clock, or are you paying her overtime?"

With a frown he glanced at his watch, obviously surprised to see it past quitting time. "I just assumed since she was still here that she was working."

That was part of the problem. Cole took Melodie's enthusiasm to do his bidding for granted. But, Jo decided, that wasn't *her* dilemma to resolve. It was up to Melodie to change her abiding, predictable ways and set Cole straight—both on a business level *and* a personal one.

Cole's blue-eyed gaze took in the fare she was enjoying and skimmed over the card that had been attached to the basket. He read the note, then smiled warmly at her from across the desk, looking like a younger version of their deceased father with his tousled sable hair, lean features, and head-turning good looks. "By the way, good job on the Faron case."

"Thanks." She accepted his compliment with pleasure and satisfaction.

When she'd quit the police force and decided she wanted to work for Cole, her brother had been reluctant to hire her, not that she could blame him. Her past actions gave him too much reason to discount her ability to defend herself, or others. But her suggestion to specialize in finding abducted and missing children was a relatively safe field that Cole eventually approved. It also added a different dimension to the agency, drew a whole new clientele, and helped her absolve the guilt she carried over a past case gone bad.

She drew a deep breath, pushed aside her thoughts, and waved a hand at the champagne and strawberries. "Care to join us for a drink to celebrate?"

He shook his head, his gaze dark and distracted. "Thanks, but I don't have time. Since Noah has made himself conveniently unavailable, I need to call Vince back and…" Cole's sentence ebbed into silence as he belatedly realized his error.

Jo perked up at the mention of the bail bond agent who traded professional favors with Cole. On occasion, Vince found himself shorthanded and needed a bail enforcement agent to retrieve someone who'd jumped bail. Cole was a certified recovery agent, as were she and Noah.

"What does Vince need?" she asked.

A scowl creased Cole's expression, which did nothing to dissuade Jo's interest. It never did. Her brother had a habit of being overprotective when it came to her. It had been that way ever since their mother had divorced their father when she was five, and she'd ended up shuffled between two households. As the oldest, Cole had taken on more duties and responsibilities than any teenager should have had to endure.

"Spill it, Cole," she said, pushing his hesitation.

His jaw unclenched, but his hold on the file folder in his hand tightened. "A guy skipped out on his bond, and I owe Vince a favor," he said with uncharacteristic nonchalance. "I traced the guy back to his Washington State residence, and I was going to ask Noah if he could recover the skip since I'm on the verge of cracking the Petrick case. But since Noah isn't around, I'll just call Vince and have him find someone else to do the job.''

Adrenaline shot through her veins. "I'll do it." Standing, she rounded the desk toward Cole.

"No."

She stopped in front of him, bristling, though she and Cole conducted this same argument every time. Her brother preferred when she kept a low profile and stayed out of trouble. For the most part, she'd been a commendable employee and sister. But she resented that he wouldn't let her do a job she was fully qualified to perform. She'd never been afraid of the chase and capture—not when she'd been a cop and not now—and she actually enjoyed an occasional run. It appeased the restlessness in her, which she'd been experiencing too much of lately. The bounty she made also helped to fund her low-income abduction cases, which was her main priority. And the well was quickly running dry to support those gratis projects she took on from time to time.

She folded her arms over her chest, refusing to back down, a stubborn trait she'd learned from the very guy standing in front of her. "You know, for someone who showed me the tricks of the trade, you certainly have a way of making me sound inept, *despite* my training.''

His gaze narrowed at her attempt to heap guilt onto his conscience. "I'm not trying to make you feel inept," he countered. "Dammit, Joelle, you shouldn't be out gallivanting after criminals. That's why you quit the police force.''

That wasn't why she'd resigned, and they both knew it. But it was a moot point she didn't wish to argue. "I need the extra money to help supplement my lower-income cases."

"*I'll* help fund those cases. I've told you that."

"No, thank you." She appreciated her brother's support, but as always she refused to accept his offer. While the agency made damn good money from locating missing persons and other investigative services, which in turn fattened her own paycheck, she didn't feel right about draining his finances, or the company's, to support her own personal cause.

Ignoring any further protests, she plucked the folder from his grasp and didn't even flinch when he growled in response. Having been raised by Cole since the age of sixteen, she knew he was more bark and growl than bite.

He dropped into the chair Melodie had recently vacated, and Jo skimmed the contents of the file without his interference. She found all the pertinent information enclosed—a bail bond agreement, a certified copy of the bail, a booking slip, a picture of the fugitive and a copy of his Washington State driver's license. Though the guy had committed his crimes in San Francisco, he apparently hadn't bothered with a California renewal.

She took in his statistics. Dean Colter, age 32. Six feet tall and one hundred and ninety-five pounds. Judging by the date of birth on the document, he'd be celebrating his thirty-third birthday behind bars, since that date was next week Friday.

Her gaze traveled between the booking photo and the one on the license, comparing the two. The man had pitch-black hair, and though the license stated his eyes were green, she couldn't confirm that with either photograph. While the driver's license showed Dean Colter with a short, executive haircut and an easy grin, the booking picture captured a grown-out shaggy hairstyle and a cocky smirk. Obviously, the former photo had been taken *before* Dean's penchant for a life of crime.

Her finger skimmed down the attached report, absorbing more details and what he'd been charged with. Grand theft auto. "This is hardly a threatening skip." She met her brother's gaze. "Come on, Cole, cut me some slack. It's not as though I'll be dealing with a murderer here." She'd certainly come up against much worse.

"How do you know?" he challenged.

She perched her jean-clad bottom on the edge of her desk. "Because it states that he's a first-time offender with no priors. How dangerous can he be?"

Cole elevated a dark brow in response. "Did you happen to notice that his bail was set at a hundred thousand dollars?"

She glanced back to confirm Cole's claim, and her jaw nearly dropped in shock. She'd definitely missed that tidbit. "Why? He was only charged with GTA. That's a felony, yes, but a minor crime in general."

"He was arrested with half a dozen high-end vehicles that were headed for a chop shop and theft ring that the local police have been trying to bust for the past three months. The guy knows the contact's name, and he was willing to testify against him. The bail was set at such a high amount to keep him honest, but being a first-timer, he was very predictable and hightailed it back to his home address in Washington."

"He's easy money then," she said, very aware that her cut would be a cool ten grand, which would go a long way in filling her professional reservoir.

Cole sighed, the sound rife with resignation. "It's a good fifteen-hour drive to Seattle from Oakland."

As if that minor inconvenience would deflate her determination! She figured out the time line in her mind. "If I leave within the hour and spend the night at a motel on the way, I'll be there by tomorrow afternoon." She flashed Cole a quick grin that reflected the tide of exhilaration blossoming within her and warded off any further argument from him. "I'll be back before the weekend is over."

She'd return with her guy in tow, and an easy ten grand in her pocket.

2

"WHAT ARE YOU STILL DOING at home?" Brett Rivers, the CEO of Colter Traffic Control asked his boss, the disapproval in his tone clearly drifting through the phone line. "You should have been long gone by now."

"Yeah, I know." Dean tucked the cordless phone more comfortably against his ear as he walked out of his master bath with everything he needed for his spontaneous getaway. Brett was his right-hand man, a good friend, and someone Dean trusted implicitly to hold down the fort in his absence. "I keep telling myself the same thing," he said, shoving his shaving kit into his duffle bag on top of the casual clothing he'd packed. "And I promise I'm almost out the door."

After three years of working day in and day out to the point of mental exhaustion and burnout, Dean was anxious to taste a bit of freedom and indulge in a week of pure relaxation and solitude—with a cold beer in one hand and a fishing pole in the other. While basking in the sun and waiting for the trout to bite, he had some serious thinking to do about his future and the direction of his father's company. To make the important decisions awaiting him, he needed a mind free and clear of any distractions or influences.

Dean gave his bedroom one last quick glance, found nothing he couldn't live without, and addressed Brett's question while zipping up his piece of luggage. "I know I told you I'd be leaving early this morning, but I had a few things to wrap up at the office and it took longer than I expected."

As soon as the words left his mouth, he groaned, realizing that he sounded just like his father, who'd passed away three years ago from a stroke. How many times had Dean been on the receiving end of that same excuse while growing up? And how many times had he resented that flippant explanation and sworn he'd never be like his father, who'd been obsessed with work to the point of excluding everything else in his life?

Too many times to count, yet here Dean was, careening down that same path to emotional and physical destruction. Sure, he had some work-related success to show for his efforts. He also had a broken engagement.

On a personal level his life was sorely lacking, and that knowledge was beginning to bother him. Especially since he'd lived such a carefree, easygoing life before taking on the family business. Hard to believe how much of a rebel he'd been back then. Now, when he came home in the evening after a twelve-hour day, or a week-long business trip, he was too aware that there was nothing or no one waiting for him. Hell, he didn't even have the time to care for a pet, let alone give attention and affection to a woman. And the truth of the matter was, what woman would endure his rigorous schedule for the long run?

Certainly not Lora, the woman he'd been engaged to before taking over the reins of Colter Traffic Control for his father—before the demands of his job had taken over his life. Since then, he'd discovered that developing something deeper than an amicable acquaintance was difficult. He didn't have the time to get to know a woman well enough to establish something more than a brief fling. Nurturing a meaningful relationship took time and energy, and after handling each day's busy, exhausting workload he depleted both.

And now, a life-altering opportunity loomed in front of him, beckoning him, tempting him to seriously consider the offer that could change the course of his future and give him his old life back. Yet years of obligations and responsibilities told him to stay firmly grounded. The decision had him torn in two.

Grabbing his duffle bag, Dean headed downstairs to the kitchen, shoving those thoughts out of his mind. He'd have plenty of free, quiet time at the lakeside cabin he'd rented to mull over those issues and make decisions.

"So, what's with the phone call?" Brett prompted. "It's Saturday, my day off, and I've got a gorgeous redhead in a short, tight dress awaiting my attention."

Dean grinned. At least his friend had his priorities straight. "I wanted to check in with you one last time before I hit the road, and wanted to let you know I put a few contracts on your desk for you to handle while I'm gone."

"Consider it done."

Dean dropped his canvas bag on the kitchen table, then loaded a small cooler with a few sodas and snacks for the drive. "Also, Clairmont Construction increased their order of arrowboards, traffic beacons and portable light towers for that repair work they've got going on the freeway. The unexpected rain has put them behind, and they're working double shifts to bring the project in on time."

"Dean, I've got it handled," Brett drawled good-naturedly. "Get the hell out of Dodge, already. By the way, are you taking any company with you?"

"Nope." He snapped the lid to the cooler shut and set the insulated container next to his bag. "It'll be just me and Mother Nature."

"Man, you have no sense of fun at all, do you?" Brett said, sounding disappointed at Dean's lack of creativity in the opposite sex department. "Give me the address of the cabin and I'll send someone to keep you occupied during the day, warm at night, and help celebrate your birthday. Trust me, you'll come back to Seattle a new man."

He'd been so caught up in work and his last business trip to San Francisco that he'd forgotten all about his birthday. Not that he normally did much more than join his friends for a drink, or have dinner with his mother. And the sad thing was, three years ago he would have jumped at the opportunity to celebrate his birthday exactly as Brett was suggesting, but now his mind was consumed with business matters.

He didn't doubt the sincerity of Brett's generous offer and was quick to set his friend straight. "Thanks, but I'd just as soon find my own woman."

After a few more minutes of ribbing from his friend to get a real life, Dean hung up the phone, shaking his head. He spent the next half hour loading his car with the cooler, camping gear, and fishing supplies he'd recently purchased through the Internet. After one final walk through the house to make sure everything was secured, he grabbed his duffle and keys from the table and headed out to the garage where his cherry-red, vintage '65 Mustang convertible awaited him.

Along with a woman holding a shotgun.

Startled to find he had company, he came to an abrupt halt. On the heels of realizing he wasn't alone came a twinge of apprehension as he warily eyed that lethal-looking weapon she cradled in one arm. Thankfully, it was pointed at the ground and not at him. She stood just where the rolling garage door opened, feet planted apart in a military type stance, and an air of boldness and presumptuousness radiating off her.

Despite the gun, she didn't *look* like a rough and tumble G.I. Jane. She wore her rich brown hair in a sleek ponytail, which served to emphasize a pretty face that seemed only to need the most basic of cosmetics to enhance her beguiling features. She was average in height, slender in stature, and undeniably feminine, but there was no mistaking she was physically fit.

He shifted on his feet and returned his gaze to her face. Her lashes blinked lazily over eyes a velvet shade of blue, and a slow, confident smile lifted one corner of her mouth.

Despite the circumstances, a warm frisson of awareness trickled through him. Damn if he didn't find all that brazen confidence sexy. And exciting. The gleam in her eye was predatory with a definite challenge, and his body responded in an instinctive way that reminded him just how long it had been since he'd had a woman in his bed. More months than he cared to recall.

Cautiously, he stepped closer to the passenger side of the car and tossed his bag in the back seat. "Can I help you?"

She moved forward slowly, her stroll deceptively casual, that intimidating shotgun gripped loosely in her hand. Her hips, encased in button-fly jeans, swayed gently with each step. The blouse overlaying a white cotton tank top fluttered open, and he experienced a jolt of surprise to catch a glimpse of silver handcuffs clipped to the waistband of her jeans.

She stopped near the trunk of the Mustang, keeping distance between them, and tipped her head inquiringly. "Are you Dean Colter?" she asked, her voice low, throaty and assuming.

She knew his name. The knowledge registered, momentarily diverting his thoughts from those handcuffs and what she intended to do with them. "Yeah, I'm

Dean Colter," he verified, suddenly feeling at a disadvantage. "And you are?"

"Jo Sommers," she supplied easily. "Your personal escort."

He frowned at her. *His personal escort?* Then his confusion ebbed as his earlier conversation with Brett tumbled through his mind. Obviously, his friend had meant what he'd said about sending him a woman for his birthday, but how had Brett arranged for her arrival so quickly?

The answer didn't really matter, not when Dean was coming to understand, and appreciate, that this woman's attire and realistic props were all part of some kind of law enforcement costume. One she'd most likely remove, piece by piece, until that luscious body was completely exposed for his eyes only. She'd said herself that she was his personal escort—a new, politically correct title for a stripper, he was guessing—sent for his pleasure and entertainment.

And he planned to cooperate.

He had no place more important to be at the moment, and his vacation could wait a few more minutes in view of the fun this gorgeous woman promised. He'd made a vow to lighten up and take life less seriously, to recapture some of the fun and spontaneity he'd enjoyed before his father's death. What could be more frivolous than playing along with her skit and enjoying the show?

She peered through the rear window to the back seat, taking in the items he'd packed for his trip, then slanted him a challenging look. "Going some-where?"

He'd go wherever she led him. Giving her his most charming, persuasive smile, he tossed out a dare of his own. "Well, now, that all depends on what *you* have in mind, sweetheart."

A slow, reciprocating smile curved her mouth. "I think you know *exactly* what I have in mind. Don't make any sudden moves, do exactly as I say, and we'll get along just fine."

Her voice was smooth, but her words were firm and commanding. Too curious to see what she intended, he held up his hands in supplication. "You've got my full cooperation."

"That's good to hear, because your cooperation will make what I've got to do much easier for the both of us." The barrel of her toy shotgun gestured him toward the back of the vehicle, closer to where she stood. "Put your hands on the trunk of the car, keep them there, and spread your legs."

His brows shot upward in surprise, but he did as she ordered. He'd expected a striptease, nothing more, but who was he to put a crimp into her presentation? Pocketing his keys, he assumed the position.

He glanced over his shoulder at her, enjoying the kind of lighthearted, playful moment so reminiscent of the wild past he'd left behind. "I take it this is where I get frisked?" he asked, attempting to inject a bit of teasing between them.

She moved behind him, bringing with her a subtle scent of something soft and feminine. "Ahh, been through this before, have you?'' Her voice held a slight cynical edge that added to the realism of her act.

"Actually, no," he replied with a grin. "But I guess there's a first time for everything."

Pressing a hand against the center of his back, she holstered her shotgun in a leather loop on her belt. "It's a standard search, Mr. Colter, just to be sure you aren't carrying any concealed weapons."

That all depends on what kind of concealed weapon you're searching for. "It's your show," he drawled, "And I'm all yours, to do with as you please."

She uttered a soft snort of laughter that stirred the hair at the back of his neck and sent a pleasurable shiver down his spine. With a booted foot tucked against his sneakered one, she widened his stance even more, then skimmed her slender hands along his shoulders and under his arms. She leaned closer to sweep her palms over his chest and abdomen, causing the lush fullness of her breasts to brush his back and her hips to graze his. Heat pooled in his groin and ignited like wildfire wherever she touched.

And she touched him *everywhere.* Impersonal, yet intimate at the same time. Her fingers dipped into the waistband of his jeans and followed the circumference around to his back where her splayed hands dragged over his back pockets. The curve of his buttocks received equal treatment, and then her thumbs followed the crease between his thighs.

He sucked in a quick breath as the tips of her fingers grazed very masculine territory. But the tantalizing caress didn't last long—just fleeting enough to tempt and tease and arouse. She continued on, those capable hands traveling down the outside length of his legs, then she squatted to pat around his ankles and smooth her palms back up the inseam of his pants, all the way to the crotch of his jeans.

And still, she wasn't done with her shameless exploration. Her hands slid around to the front of his thighs, checking the contents of his pockets through denim by grasping the material. She came into contact with his keys and loose change, and moved toward the fly of his jeans.

Every molecule in his body tensed, including that inherently male part of him she was about to frisk. He felt compelled to issue a warning. "If you're not careful, sweetheart, you're gonna end up finding the only concealed weapon I've got on me."

"Luckily for you I'm trained in handling firearms." Her sultry voice, laced with wry humor, drifted into his ear from behind him. "And I haven't had one accidentally discharge on me yet." She proved her claim by handling him gently and efficiently, finishing her search with quick precision.

An amused chuckle rumbled up from Dean's chest. Not only was Jo Sommers gorgeous and sexy, but she was witty and sassy, too. Obviously, Brett had known she was exactly what he needed to alleviate the stress and seriousness that had consumed his life for too long.

She grasped his left hand from the car and brought

it behind his back. Before he could ask what she meant to do, he felt cool metal encircle his wrist and snap tight. She repeated the process with his other hand, restricting both of his arms with those handcuffs he'd seen earlier.

Then she turned him around to face her, and he wriggled his wrists to see if they'd pop free from the toy handcuffs, only to discover that the metal shackles were the real thing. He came to the immediate conclusion that he didn't like being restrained, even if it was part of this stripper's routine.

"You know, there really is no need for the cuffs," he said with a flirtatious grin. "I surrender willingly."

She gave him an assessing, head-to-toe glance. "You seem like a really nice guy, and you've been more cooperative than most, but I don't take chances with anyone. This is standard procedure."

Her words didn't make sense. With her warm fingers firmly grasping his elbow, she ushered him out of the garage and down the driveway toward the black Suburban that waited at the curb. A pleasant afternoon breeze riffled through his hair, contrasting with the unease trickling through him.

Had he misjudged this entire situation?

He was beginning to suspect he had, yet he couldn't figure out her angle. If she was a stripper, she should have been down to a G-string and a come-hither smile by now.

"Mind me asking where we're going?" he asked, displaying a casualness he didn't completely feel.

She didn't slow her long-legged stride, her silky

ponytail bouncing against her shoulders with each determined step. "You know exactly where we're going."

"No, I don't."

She didn't seem inclined to believe him or answer his original question. Reaching the passenger side of the vehicle, she opened the door. With a hand on top of his head and her body crowding his in a very stalwart manner, she assisted him into the seat. He slipped inside and sat there for a few seconds, too dumbfounded and confused to do otherwise.

What the hell was going on?

She grabbed the seat belt and leaned over him, dragging the nylon strap across his lap to click it into place by his hip, her movements quick and economical. Too late, he realized how defenseless he was with his hands manacled behind his back, how completely at this woman's mercy he was. Normally, that wouldn't be a cause for concern, but he was rapidly coming to understand that this scenario wasn't the fun and games he'd originally thought Brett had sent his way.

His gut churned with apprehension as he stared into her brilliant blue eyes. Up close, he could see the rich gold that rimmed her irises. "You're not a stripper, are you?"

She braced a hand on the doorframe, a delicately arched brow winging upward. "Did you *hire* a stripper?"

Irritation shot through him. "No." He winced at the unintentional bite to his voice, but couldn't deny he was suddenly on edge. "My birthday is next week, on Friday, and I thought a friend of mine might have sent you."

She laughed lightly, his wrong assumption obviously a source of entertainment for her. "I'm sorry to disappoint you and spoil your birthday plans, but all my clothes are staying in place."

What a shame. "Then what do you want with me?"

Crossing her arms over her chest, she stared at him for a long moment, scrutinizing him with a penetrating stare. "I'm a bail recovery agent, Mr. Colter," she finally said. "And I'm taking you back to San Francisco to stand trial for grand theft auto."

His mouth fell open, then snapped shut again, jarring his teeth with the impact. "Grand theft auto?" he repeated, unable to keep the high-pitched incredulity from his voice. His mind grappled with the concept of this sensual, slender woman being a bounty hunter, and him the fugitive, but the notion was too ridiculous to comprehend.

It would have been a nice sexual fantasy, if the reality of his predicament wasn't so damned unnerving.

He took a deep calming breath and tried to keep his perspective on the situation. "I swear I have no idea what you're talking about."

She gave him a placating look as she withdrew the shotgun from its sheath on her belt. "Sure you don't."

This time, Dean found her weapon much more intimidating than the toy gun he'd originally assumed she carried for the act that wasn't an act. That "toy" could've blown a hole straight through him.

Christ, she was carting him off to jail! The realization made his stomach cramp. Most likely, he'd be spending a night in a cold cell until his lawyers could sort out this mess. Perspiration beaded on his forehead, despite the cool May afternoon. Disbelief warred with more urgent emotions—like making her understand that this was one big, huge mistake.

"Lady, you've got the wrong guy," he tried to reason.

Reaching behind his seat, she set the weapon on the floorboard, then straightened and released a sigh laced with impatience. "By your own admittance you're Dean Colter, this is the residence I've got on file for you, and you fit the profile I have with me." She shrugged. "That's all the evidence I need to take you back to San Francisco."

Before he could argue further, she slammed the door on his heated retort and strutted back toward his house, leaving him to wonder how in the hell he'd gotten himself into such a mess.

More importantly, how was he going to get out of it?

3

SHE'D CAUGHT DEAN COLTER just in time. Judging by the camping paraphernalia Jo discovered in his car, she surmised that he'd been on the verge of fleeing again. Another ten minutes, and he would have left nothing but a cold trail in his wake.

Yes, success was sweet, indeed.

After executing a quick search of his vehicle, she grabbed his duffle from the back seat, set the bag on the trunk of the car, and unzipped it. She rifled through the contents for weapons, drugs, or anything else illegal she had no desire to transport across two state lines and found nothing but clothes and personal items. The most lethal thing he had on him was a razor for shaving. The front pocket held his wallet, and she flipped it open, inventorying credit cards, cash, and a Washington State driver's license confirming everything she already knew about Dean Colter.

The guy was completely clean—and one of the most accommodating skips she'd ever encountered. The beanbag shotgun she'd armed herself with had been a formality, not a necessity. There had been no foot chase or struggle, no use of force or violence, just a ridiculously easy capture that made this job, and the cash she'd make once she turned in Dean Colter to the authorities, the easiest money she'd ever deposited into her savings account.

Of course it had helped tremendously that he believed she'd been a stripper sent as a birthday gift, she thought with an amused grin. His guileless assumption explained his flirtatious behavior when she'd first arrived, his carefree acquiescence in obeying her orders, and his easy compliance as she'd frisked him.

But that in no way explained her own startling reaction to Dean Colter, she thought with a frown as she stuffed his wallet back into the front pocket of his duffle. She'd been professional and sensible during her body search—until he'd made that playful comment about her finding his only concealed weapon and she'd countered with her own cheeky retort.

It had been an automatic reply, one she'd regretted as soon as the words had left her mouth. And much to her own chagrin, she hadn't been able to stem the awareness that had flooded her in the aftermath of that careless, shameless rejoinder. Suddenly, patting him down had become more than a professional duty.

The man had a nice body—not overtly muscular, but athletically built with wide shoulders, toned arms and a lean waist and belly. His thighs had been rock hard, his buttocks nicely rounded and defined. And when her hands had brushed over the fly of his jeans and felt his reaction to her search, she hadn't been able to stop the tide of heat that had suffused her veins and settled in places it had no business settling. Even now, the recollection had the ability to make her pulse pick up its beat.

Get a grip, Sommers. Dean Colter might be good-looking, charming, and likeable despite his recent rap sheet, but she'd *never* lusted over a guy she'd taken into custody. Hell, she couldn't remember the last man who'd even prompted such instantaneous lust, which made her reckless response to Dean all the more perplexing. He might not be a murderer, but he was a felon nonetheless.

She could only blame her actions and reactions on exhaustion, she reasoned as she checked the entrance to the house to make sure the door was locked. She'd pushed herself to get here before sundown, taking minimal breaks along the drive. Although she'd met her goal, she'd only gotten five hours of sleep the night before when she was someone who needed a good, solid eight—or more. After ten hours on the road today with two more to go, she was not only fatigued, but obviously a little loopy, too.

Or just too damned sexually deprived.

She snorted at that, but suspected there was a kernel of truth in the sentiment. But no matter what her excuse, she'd do well to remember that she had a job to accomplish—one that had no room for the kind of distraction Dean Colter posed. She needed her guard up and her psyche alert.

Duffle bag in hand, she hit the switch that controlled the garage door, then ran out. The rolling metal panel doors clanged shut behind her seconds after her retreat, and she headed down the driveway to her vehicle, anxious to be on her way again.

Her captive didn't seem as flirtatious and carefree now that he realized what an error in judgment he'd made with her. In fact, the scowl creasing his features as he stared out the passenger window watching her approach clearly reflected his displeasure.

She circled around the back of the Suburban, tossed his bag into the back seat, then slid behind the wheel. A loud "click" echoed in the vehicle as she took her usual precaution and activated all the door locks from the control panel on the armrest.

"So, where were you off to before I showed up?" she asked, wanting to gauge his mood and what kind of personality she'd be dealing with before she hit the road.

Her prisoners usually fell into one of three categories of behavior during the transport back to jail: belligerent and verbally abusive; brooding and opting for the silent treatment; or attempting to reason with her and trying to validate their innocence.

Dean wasn't happy about the situation, but one look into his clear, striking green eyes and she knew she could rule out the first scenario. There was no malice in his gaze, just a wealth of frustration. His inexperience and first-time felon charge obviously hadn't jaded him. Yet.

"I was on my way to a much-needed week-long vacation at a secluded cabin in the mountains."

The gear she'd found in his car certainly verified

his claim. She appreciated his honesty, though she thought the "much needed" part stretched credibility. "That would have been a good place to hide out," she agreed, snapping on her seat belt. "I'm sorry to put a crimp in your plans."

He shifted in his seat, managing to turn those wide shoulders her way so he was looking at her straight-on. His presence was potently male and more than she'd bargained for, filling the interior of the large cab with an enticing masculine heat and scent she hadn't anticipated having to deal with. The combination aroused her senses and stirred something vital deep in her belly.

Hunger, she told herself, startled by the unexpected fluttering sensation she'd experienced. A craving for *food,* not something totally forbidden to her. She'd skipped lunch and had only munched on a chocolate-covered granola bar she'd brought along for the ride, and her stomach was making its needs known.

That's all it was, she assured herself.

Dean's gaze was direct as it connected with hers, his expression businesslike. "Look, Ms. Sommers, I think there's been some kind of mistake."

Here we go, she thought. Reality was finally settling in, and he was grasping at any excuse to gain back his freedom. Unfortunately, the argument he'd chosen was particularly overused, and a feeble one at that.

Unclipping the set of keys from the waistband of her jeans, she inserted one into the ignition. She actually felt a twinge of sympathy for him. He seemed so green about this entire process—or maybe he was dreading the return trip to San Francisco to testify against the leader of an auto theft ring. That would definitely explain the inkling of desperation she detected beneath his more confident facade.

"Mr. Colter, this isn't a mistake." Surprised to hear the regret in her own voice, she quickly replaced it with indifference. "Your arrest is as real as it gets. I have the paperwork to prove it."

At the sound of the engine turning over, a touch of panic flared to life in his eyes. "Don't I have any rights?" he demanded. The handcuffs behind him clanked together as his arms and shoulders flexed from their unnatural position. The corded muscles in his biceps bulged, drawing her gaze as they strained against the short sleeves of his knit shirt.

Impressive muscles she'd be a fool to underestimate—no matter how much they, or the man, fascinated her.

"I have to have *some* kind of rights," he reiterated when she didn't immediately answer him. "A phone call to my attorney, at the very least, to sort out this misunderstanding?"

She shook her head, which helped to gain her bearings and remove her traitorous gaze from his physique. "You forfeited all your rights when you jumped bail. You can call your attorney, or anyone else you want, when you're back in jail."

Exasperation clenched his jaw and radiated off him in waves. "I want to see that information you *claim* to have on me," he said abruptly, just as she reached for the gear shift to put the vehicle in Drive. "Is *that* within my rights?"

He sounded so indignant, she had to bite the inside of her cheek to keep from grinning. She recognized his appeal for the stall tactic it was, but decided to grant him this one small concession which would only take a few minutes out of her time. Besides, in her experience, she'd always found that being faced with irrefutable facts had a way of making a person much more accommodating, and much less argumentative.

And there was no refuting the incriminating evidence she had on Dean Colter.

"I'd be happy to show you the information." Smiling sweetly, she withdrew the pocket folder she'd tucked between her seat and the console, then pulled out the file nestled within containing all the pertinent reports, releases and documents she had on him.

"You could have killed me with that shotgun you were carrying, you know," he said, his tone rough with censure.

"What?" His abrupt change of topic threw her off-kilter, and she looked up from sorting through the papers to find his expression disapproving, and his full lips thinned into a flattened line. Then it dawned on her what he was referring to. "Oh, that wasn't a shotgun. Not a real one, anyway."

He gaped at her. "You go around confronting people with a *toy* gun?"

Her stomach clenched, and her hands grew cold and clammy as unexpected memories swamped her...of a pistol trembling in her hands, her frantic shouts to the perp she'd cornered to drop his gun, and ultimately her inability to follow through with the threat he'd posed, to her and her partner. Then two simultaneous gunshots—one the perp's, the other Brian's.

She winced at the awful recollection, which still remained so sharp and fresh in her mind—as if the life-altering incident had happened yesterday instead of two years ago. The revolver holstered at her side felt like a two-ton weight, reminding her of failures, disappointments and the heart-wrenching burden she'd have to live with forever.

Yes, she carried a *real* gun with her, but she wouldn't draw it unless she absolutely had to. Because now she knew if she drew her weapon, she'd put herself in the position of having to fire the gun. And she doubted her ability to do so, more than she feared protecting herself with less deadly forces.

She swallowed to ease the tightness closing up her throat. "It's a beanbag shotgun," she replied, her voice still tight from those grim memories of the past. At his questioning stare, she explained. "It would have brought you to an immediate halt, possibly knocked you on your ass, and no doubt have given you a nasty bruise, but you would have lived."

"I'm so relieved," he drawled sarcastically.

She shrugged. "You're certainly no good to me dead," she said, adopting a flippant attitude.

A huff of disbelieving laughter escaped him at her sassy reply. Feeling a smile tug the corner of her mouth, she ducked her head and trained her thoughts back to the file. Spreading the folder open on his lap, she allowed him a quiet moment to read the bail bond and authorization form, as well as look over the photographs the bondsman had provided.

His gaze narrowed and a frown formed as he glanced from the unflattering mug shot to the picture on the copy of his driver's license. He examined each one, back and forth, his intense scrutiny causing her own gaze to drift to the photographs to do her own idle comparison.

Without a doubt, the men in each picture resembled two different personas. But their coloring and features were so similar it was difficult to refute that they were one and the same. In both photos, Dean was cited as having green eyes, and the man in front of her definitely had those...gorgeous, sexy green eyes she'd seen darken with desire earlier, and flash with annoyance moments ago. Both images possessed pitch-black hair, and it was clear to her that the man sitting beside her owned a head of thick hair as dark as a raven's wing.

Somewhere between his booking photo and today, he'd gotten a haircut, changing back to his short, neat style—an executive cut with the longer strands on top falling into soft, precision layers that invited a woman to touch and feel.

And she had.

She'd gained intimate knowledge of just how silky and warm those strands were—could still remember the velvet texture and warm feel as those locks had sifted through her fingers when she'd touched his head to guide him into the car. Could still recall the shimmering awareness that had taken up residence within her with that brief contact.

The only thing she couldn't find any resemblance to was the cocky, arrogant smirk on the face of the man in the booking photo. Her instincts stirred. She'd yet to see that side of the Dean Colter she'd cuffed—the flirtatious, charming guy who'd only revealed a few bouts of ire and frustration, and not the aggression she would have expected judging by the conceited expression in the mug shot. If contrasting personality traits gave her a second's pause, then it was the glaring evidence Dean himself had provided that brought everything back into perspective.

He'd openly declared to being Dean Colter.

"Unbelievable," he muttered, looking both stunned and confused when he glanced back up at her.

"I take it you've seen enough?"

He didn't answer. Instead, he drew a deep breath and slowly exhaled it. The file balanced on his thighs started to slip, and she made a grab for the folder, then returned the information to its spot next to her seat.

"You've got the wrong guy, Jo."

His voice was quiet, eerily so, causing a distinct shiver to ripple down her spine. No pleading. No begging. Just a statement of fact that discounted everything he'd just read. His eyes had turned a shade of green so startling clear and sincere they made her *want* to believe him.

But she knew better than to be conned, no matter how convincing his act. She wouldn't underestimate the power of his charms and attempts to persuade her. "Oh, now that's original. If I had a dollar for every time I heard that line as a cop I'd be a very rich girl."

He stared at her for a moment in amazement. "You're a cop?"

"I *was*," she said, seeing no reason why she shouldn't answer his question. Between tonight's two-hour jaunt and tomorrow's long drive, they'd be confined to this vehicle for fifteen hours, and she didn't mind making polite talk as opposed to putting up with brooding silence. "I quit the force two years ago."

"To pursue a career in bounty hunting?"

More astonishment, and the way he was looking at her...taking in her ponytail, her features, then taking quick inventory of the rest of her body before returning to her face. She suppressed the warm glow that followed in the wake of his thorough assessment.

"I work for my brother as a P.I." Putting the Suburban in gear, she pulled away from the curb and eased onto the road. "I specialize in missing persons and abductions, but I do the occasional bail recovery on the side to make extra money."

He looked back at his house as they drove away and left his sanctuary behind. "Bail recovery?" He snorted derisively. "This is kidnapping, you know."

"Kidnapping?" She rolled her eyes and flipped on the air-conditioning to low, welcoming the cool rush of air that billowed across her skin. "Not according to the information you just read."

"I'm not that guy!" he said through gritted teeth.

Would he never give up? "I looked through your wallet in your duffle," she told him. "Not only do you say you're Dean Colter, so does your license."

He blew out a frustrated stream of breath. "I *am* Dean Colter, but I'm not the guy in that mug shot."

"Oh, I believe you," she said drolly as she headed out of the residential area and back to the interstate. "But it's the judge you're gonna have to convince, not me."

His lip curled sullenly and, unable to do otherwise, he settled back into his seat. "Great," he muttered as he stared out the window moodily. "Just great."

She made a right-hand turn up the I-5 on-ramp and moved over to the fast lane, leaving Seattle behind. "Why don't you just relax and enjoy the trip?"

"It's kinda hard to relax when these damned handcuffs are stabbing into my back and my arms are falling asleep," he grumbled.

Poor baby. "If you flatten your palms against the seat it'll relieve some of the pressure."

"And if you took off the handcuffs it would relieve some of the pain."

"Sorry," she said, not sounding the least bit contrite. "But I can't risk my safety for your comfort."

He heaved a gut-deep sigh. "So I've got to be trussed up like this all the way to San Francisco?"

"Pretty much." She reached for the trip ticket she'd tucked into the visor, which mapped her drive back to San Francisco and the places she planned to stop along the way. Giving it a cursory glance while watching the road, she pegged her next destination as Kelso, Washington. "I've been on the road since six this morning. We'll be stopping in a few hours to get a hotel for the night, and I'll let you stretch your arms then. We'll get something to eat, too."

"A free meal. At least I get something out of this trip." The slightest bit of humor had returned to his voice, as if he'd resigned himself to the inevitable. "And just be warned, I skipped lunch today and I'm starved."

The way he said the word *starved,* with a low, rumbling growl in the back of his throat, brought a whole new meaning to the word.

Apparently, his appetite matched her own.

BEING HAULED to San Francisco by a female bounty hunter wasn't exactly the vacation Dean had envisioned, but as the chasm between Seattle and him widened, he decided he had no choice but to improvise and be adventurous.

Spontaneity. Relaxation. Being impetuous. All nuances of his old life he missed. That had been part of the reason he'd decided to take a vacation in the first place, based on the startling realization that he was fast on his way to becoming a workaholic like his father had been. Putting the company before himself was something he'd sworn he'd never do, yet he'd spent the past three years doing exactly that, to the extent that he was teetering on the verge of burnout.

Not only did he need the time away from work to think about the fate of Colter Traffic Control and his future, but it had been too long since he'd put himself, and his desires, first.

And there was no doubt he desired Jo Sommers. Despite having no idea how he'd gotten himself into this mess, this sexy, spirited woman intrigued him. Aroused him. Fascinated him. And it had been a long time since any woman had captured his interest so thoroughly.

Whether he liked it or not, he was on this wild ride for the duration, until they reached San Francisco, his attorney was contacted, and the authorities realized they had the wrong guy and cleared his name. He couldn't deny that the driver's license and information that Jo had shown him was his, but the guy in the mug shot was *not* him, though there was enough of a resemblance to draw the conclusion that they were one and the same.

This had to be a huge misunderstanding of some sort, one he obviously couldn't explain or find a logical reason for, but it was still a mistake. One he wanted to remedy. And he had two days to figure out a way to convince Jo that he was an innocent man. The challenge was more than he could resist.

He might have lost his vacation, but he'd just gained something far more exciting and fun. The way he figured things, he had two options during this trip—resist or surrender—and being a willing and accommodating captive for Jo would be a far more pleasurable experience. To his advantage, no one would miss him or worry about his absence, since everyone believed he was off to the mountains for a week of quiet and solitude.

He was a guy who'd always made the best of a bad situation. This mishap would be no exception.

But first, he needed to make amends for his earlier grumpy behavior. Resting his head on the back of the seat, he let it roll to the side until he was looking at Jo's profile. The sun was just beginning to set on the horizon and the pastel hues made her smooth complexion shimmer with radiant warmth.

"I want to apologize for my attitude," he said, breaking the silence that had descended over the cab the past half hour. "I'm sure after I'm cleared of all charges and they find the guy who impersonated me I'll find this abduction all very humorous."

She slanted him a dubious look. "You think so?"

"It's what I keep telling myself." He blinked lazily. "You really do have my full cooperation. I've resigned myself to the fact that I can't prove my innocence until we reach the authorities, so I plan to enjoy the ride." *And you.*

The corners of her mouth curled upward, drawing his gaze to her full, luscious lips. "I like your *new* attitude."

"I like your smile," he countered honestly.

Said smile faltered self-consciously. "Thank you."

He suppressed a grin of his own. "You're welcome."

He couldn't help notice the flush on her skin. His unexpected compliment had caught her off guard, and he admitted he liked having that slight advantage. "Are you married?"

She paused, absently ran her tongue across her bottom lip, then admitted, "No."

"Can't say I'm surprised." When she gave him a quick, care-to-explain look, he shrugged his rapidly stiffening shoulders and said, "It's hard to imagine a husband allowing his wife to work as a bounty hunter."

She released a *pfft* sound of derision and rolled her eyes at what she obviously thought was an antiquated viewpoint.

"How about a boyfriend?"

She shot him a pointed look and visibly bristled. "No, and I'd appreciate it if you kept your added commentary about that to yourself," she warned.

His mouth twitched, then spilled over with the amusement he could no longer contain. Obviously, there was something about mixing a significant other with her occupation that was a source of contention for her, and he was curious to know why. He wanted to know everything he could discover about Jo Sommers—her job, why she did what she did, and the sensuality he detected simmering just beneath her tough facade.

Yeah, especially that.

Physically, he might be restrained. Mentally and verbally he was not.

The wicked possibilities were alluring and endless. He'd wanted his old life back, and here was his chance to embrace a little bit of fun.

4

A LITTLE OVER AN HOUR later, Jo pulled off the interstate and into the drive-through of a fast-food restaurant in Kelso, Washington, located next to the roadside motor lodge she planned to stay at for the night. The town was small and quiet, which suited her just fine since she wasn't looking for excitement or entertainment. All she wanted was food in her stomach, a long, hot shower to ease the tense muscles across her shoulders, a good night's rest, and total cooperation from her fugitive.

Since leaving Seattle and promising to be on his best behavior, Dean had held true to his word and been an exemplary prisoner. Then again, there wasn't much trouble he could get into being handcuffed and strapped securely into his seat.

There were no more protests of not being the man she sought, no more complaints about being restrained, and no more frustration underscoring his tone. Just light, comfortable conversation—mostly about her and questions about her time as a cop, the stories of which he'd found fascinating and amusing—mixed in with an occasional flirtatious comment that filled her with too much awareness. Much to her surprise, she'd actually enjoyed their easy exchange, and the time and miles had passed quickly.

She brought the vehicle to a stop in front of the large, lighted outdoor menu, keeping her window rolled up while they perused the available entrees. Deciding on what she wanted to eat, she turned and glanced at Dean, who was still looking over the selection. "What would you like?"

His deep green eyes found hers, and an irresistible grin creased the corners of his mouth. "Well, since the meals are on you, I'll have two of the double western bacon cheeseburgers, a supersize order of fries, and a supersize Coke."

Her brows rose in disbelief at the amount of food he was ordering. "Is that all?" she drawled, wondering where in the heck he planned to put the small feast. His lean belly didn't look big enough to hold two burgers at one time, let alone everything else he planned to consume.

His broad shoulders rolled in an attempt at a shrug, and his biceps flexed with the awkward movement. He winced, a clear indication that his muscles had grown stiff and sore during the drive. Still, not one derogatory word or a plea to release his cuffs slipped past his lips. "Hey, I warned you that I was starved."

So he had, and she'd obviously underestimated the voracious appetite he'd claimed to have. "Are you sure you wouldn't want some dessert to go with your supersize dinner?" she asked, a light, teasing note threading her voice.

He glanced at the menu again. "Now that you mention it, I'll take a slice of that chocolate mousse cake they're advertising.''

She'd been joking. He was completely serious, and all she could think was that he must burn a whole lot of energy if he ate like that on a regular basis. As her gaze drifted over that toned, virile body she'd patted down earlier, various ways of burning calories came to mind. The unbidden images that formed had little to do with conventional exercise, and more to do with the workout provided by hot, hard, sweaty sex...two slick bodies straining, hips pumping, thighs clenching, pulses racing uncontrollably...

Oh, yeah, her pulse had most definitely picked up its tempo. Her own body throbbed in cadence with the erotic visions that had flitted through her head, and the interior of the vehicle grew warm, despite the air-conditioning blowing cool air across her skin. She was shocked at her provocative thoughts and the path they'd traveled...and who she'd allowed to be the male lead in her sexual fantasy.

Her hands tightened on the steering wheel as she inhaled a slow breath. *Get a grip, Joelle. The man is a felon, no matter how gorgeous, sexy, and charming he might be, no matter how convincing and genuine he seems.* No matter that she'd been way too long without a man to ease the kind of sensual cravings that had recently taken up residence within her.

He wasn't a man to trust, or even lust after—not when he was on his way to jail and a future destined to be spent behind bars. Chanting that reminder silently in her head, she rolled her window down, placed his enormous, supersize order and opted for a chicken Caesar salad and an iced tea for herself.

Less than ten minutes later, without any mishaps at the restaurant's pickup window and her mind firmly back on business, she pulled the Suburban into the motor lodge parking area. After circling the lot once, she chose an isolated spot far enough away from the registration office and anyone exiting the two-story, U-shaped structure.

Turning off the engine, she withdrew the keys, unlatched her seat belt, and grabbed her wallet from the console. She cast a quick glance Dean's way, making sure he was still trussed up and immobile. "I'll be right back," she told him, satisfied that he was still firmly restrained. "I'm going to get us a room for the night and we'll eat once we're settled inside."

He flashed another one of his easygoing grins. "I'll be right here, waiting."

She opened her door and slid out of her seat, biting back a smile at his obliging attitude, as if it were *his* choice to sit tight while she was gone, and that he'd enjoy every minute of the wait. Amused with his pleasant disposition despite his predicament, she locked him into the truck and engaged the alarm.

She walked briskly across the half-full parking lot and into the small, glass-enclosed office that enabled her to keep an eye on the Suburban and Dean while she registered and paid for their one-night stay. Per her request to the night clerk, she was able to secure a room with two double beds on the first level, located around the backside of the lodge where they'd be afforded a semblance of privacy.

The transaction went smoothly, and without any trouble from Dean in the car. She drove the vehicle around the building, parked in the designated slot in front of their motel room door, and within minutes she had everything unloaded—including Dean, their duffle bags, and their food. After securing all the locks on the metal door and switching on the cool air to clear out the stuffiness, she turned her full attention to her silent, patient prisoner standing in the middle of the room.

Alone in such a confined space and surrounded by an intimate setting that included two beds, the size of him registered in a purely feminine way. When she'd first cornered him in his garage, she'd been running on pure adrenaline, ready for action and focused on apprehending him. Now, she was keenly aware of how potently male he was with those big, wide shoulders and toned arms that would have no problem wrapping around a woman her size. Then there were his lean hips encased in soft denim to consider, and strong thighs that framed impressive male anatomy. His stance was completely relaxed, his gaze warm and sensual. He gave no indication that he was wired and ready to spring to action at the first opportune moment, an attitude she'd come to expect from most of her captives.

He was tall, too—a good six inches bigger than her own five-foot-five stature that qualified her as *petite,* a word she'd hated from the moment she'd learned what it meant to the male gender—small, delicate, and a featherweight, a nickname Noah always loved to torment her with. The continual comparison of how small she was had been partly responsible for her determination as a teenager to break free from her brothers' overprotectiveness. That same fierce perseverance had followed her into her adult years as she'd struggled to prove herself as a capable law enforcement officer to her family and colleagues.

Unfortunately, while she'd proven her physical strength, agility, and endurance, she'd failed miserably at the emotional and mental fortitude she'd needed to do her job—a personal failure that had ended up costing her Brian's life.

Those thick, black lashes framing slumberous eyes blinked lazily at her. "Food's getting cold, sweetheart," Dean said, his tone a low, rich murmur in the quiet room. "And I'm getting hungrier by the second. Are you going to take off the cuffs, or do I get to enjoy the pleasure of you hand-feeding me?"

He sounded like he wouldn't have minded the latter. Refusing to allow her misbehaving thoughts to travel in that direction, she glanced around the room once more and considered her options—and performing the intimate task of feeding Dean Colter by hand was *not* one of them. Finding the small, rectangular table between the second bed and the corner of the wall, she made her decision based on Dean's consistent, non-violent behavior since she'd picked him up.

"One of the cuffs stays on at all times," she said, unwilling to compromise on that issue. "I'll secure the other handcuff around the metal pole beneath the table which will free up your other hand so you can feed *yourself*. It's more slack than I normally offer my prisoners, so don't make me regret my generosity.''

"Yes, ma'am," he drawled.

She followed that up with a steely warning. "One false move and not only will you be flat on your ass from my beanbag shotgun, but you'll remain shackled and permanently disabled for the duration of the trip—hands *and* feet. Do you understand?''

He nodded amicably, agreeing to her terms. "Sure do.''

With that assurance, she splayed a hand against his back and guided him forward, then eased him into the chair on the far side of the table. Quickly and efficiently she unfastened the metal bracelet on his right hand, then reached beneath the Formica surface and secured his left wrist to the thick metal pole. As an added precaution, she wedged him into the corner with the table by pushing it up against both sides of the walls.

Stepping back, she shrugged out of the blouse she wore over her tank top, exposing the revolver holstered to her left side that he hadn't known she carried—if the sudden raising of his brows were any indication. Tossing the gauzy garment onto the nearby bed, she unsnapped the leather strap to free the weapon as an added intimidation tactic, though her stomach rolled at the thought of having to withdraw or use the gun. Especially on Dean, whom she truly liked, despite his criminal status.

His gaze traveled from the gun to her face, his initial surprise replaced by something far more playful. "And here I thought I was the only one with a concealed weapon," he teased, a slow smile easing across his lips. "Is that thing loaded?"

His sexy innuendo was reminiscent of the provocative banter that had passed between them when she'd patted him down in his garage—before he'd realized that her cop act was for real. "I do believe that's *my* line," she shot right back.

"Touché," he acknowledged, then groaned in relief as he rolled his stiff shoulders and shook out his cramped arms. "My hands were starting to tingle and fall asleep. Thank you for releasing me," he said gratefully, then flashed her a sinful smile. "Though I have to admit that I was really looking forward to being hand-fed. You're taking all the fun out of this captive fantasy for me, Jo."

She rolled her eyes at his outrageous, flirtatious comment, then retrieved their bags of food and drinks from the dresser and slipped into her own seat across from him. "What can I say? Fulfilling fantasies isn't in my job description, and fun isn't a top priority for me when I'm on assignment."

"Too bad, on both accounts." Feigned disappointment touched his voice as he reached into a bag with his free hand for one of his double western bacon cheeseburgers and supersize fries. "So, you're an all work and no play kind of girl?"

She poured the container of Caesar dressing over her salad. "Yeah, something like that. Too much work and not enough time for play."

Which was her own fault, she knew. For the past few years she'd deliberately made work her sanctuary, a convenient way to dull the pain of the past that seemed to be her constant companion. Her cases kept her mind focused and her emotions sane...yet those same assignments were also responsible for keeping her secluded in an office during the day and crawling into a cold, lonely bed at night. Single and very much alone, if she didn't count the awful nightmares that sometimes woke her in the darkest recesses of the night and haunted her until the break of dawn.

He considered her remark for a moment as he took a big bite out of his burger and chewed. "Seems you and I have something in common."

She stabbed a forkful of lettuce and cast him a dubious glance. A cop turned P.I. and a felon couldn't be more opposite in her opinion, no matter how attractive, sexy, and tempting said felon was. "Now *that's* hard to imagine."

"No, really, we do," he insisted. Tearing open a small pouch of ketchup with the edge of his straight white teeth, he squirted the sauce onto the wax paper liner so he could dip his fries. "Too much work and not enough time for play is exactly the reason why I was taking off for a week in the mountains. And I have to tell you, Brett is going to get one hell of a good laugh when I tell him how I spent my vacation and how I mistook you as my birthday surprise."

She squeezed lemon into her iced tea and stirred the amber liquid with her straw. "Again, I'm sorry to have disappointed you."

"I'm not disappointed, Jo," he said softly, then shook his head. "Let me rephrase that. Yeah, I'm disappointed that I didn't get the show I was expecting, but my birthday isn't for another six days, and I'm still hopeful." He winked at her.

Heat suffused her skin at the thought of being this man's private stripper and slowly, gradually peeling away layers of clothing while he watched with those intense green eyes of his. "Only in your dreams, Colter."

The metal cuff around his left wrist clanged beneath the table as he leaned forward in his seat. "I'd be happy to share the details of tonight's dreams with you tomorrow morning if you'd like."

Judging by the wicked gleam in his gaze, there was no mistaking what visions would be dancing in his mind once his head hit the pillow—the very same provocative images she'd just visualized herself. "You can spare me the details, thank you very much." Plucking a piece of grilled chicken from her salad, she bit into the tender meat and rerouted the direction of their conversation. "So, who is Brett?"

"He's one of my best friends, and he also works for me." Swiping three french fries into the pool of ketchup, he popped the trio into his mouth, then took a hefty drink of his soda.

She stared at him for a long moment as she mentally analyzed his statement and came to the most logical conclusion. "So, the two of you are partners in crime and steal cars together?"

He chuckled, though she couldn't imagine what he found so humorous. "No, Brett's the CEO of my company, Colter Traffic Control."

"Really?" she drawled, wondering what kind of story he was trying to concoct. "Interesting name for a company, unless it's a front for the cars you've stolen."

A heavy sigh unraveled out of him. "No matter what you might believe about me, no matter what those police reports say or how similar I look to that guy in that mug shot you showed me, I'm not a thief." A sudden impish look passed across his features. "Well, not when it comes to cars, anyway. When I was seven I stole a pack of Juicy Fruit gum from the grocery store. When I got home and my mother found out what I'd done, she immediately took me back to face the store manager and return what I'd taken. After the lecture I got about shoplifting and being prosecuted to the full extent of the law, which terrified me at the time, I swore I'd never steal anything ever again. And I haven't. Gum or otherwise."

She smiled, and pushed her salad around on her plastic dish in search of more chicken. "Cute story, but you have to admit that 'Colter Traffic Control' sounds like a clever way of saying that your solution to controlling traffic is by taking high-dollar cars off the road so they can be taken to a chop shop or sold to a foreign market."

"Interesting theory, Ms. P.I.," he agreed, unwrapping his second burger to devour, "but totally off the mark, I'm afraid. 'Traffic Control' is the name of the company I inherited from my father when he died a few years ago."

He seemed so serious, his story almost too well-thought-out for a first-time felon. She wondered how far he planned to take this charade, and was curious enough to play along to see what he revealed. "Since you claim the business is legit, what, exactly, does your company do?"

He held up a finger to ask for a minute as he chewed the big bite he'd just taken, and she figured he needed the extra time to invent something believable. Done with most of her salad, she pushed the plate aside and rested her arms on the table, waiting for his explanation.

"Sorry 'bout that," he apologized when he could speak again, then swiped his napkin across that full, sensual mouth of his. "We rent, lease, and sell traffic control devices to general contractors for highway and freeway projects."

She had to give him extra points for originality. "Devices such as?" she prompted, certain she'd eventually back him into a corner that would leave him stammering for answers.

"Highway medians and barriers, traffic lights, signals and divider cones, parking meters, and even those big lighted signs they use during freeway construction to reroute traffic," he replied easily. Finished with his dinner, he sucked a smudge of sauce from his thumb, then opened the lid on his chocolate mousse cake. "Those are just a few of the more popular items we supply."

Propping her elbows on the table, she rested her chin on her laced fingers. "And supplying these traffic control items is such a stressful job that you needed a week-long vacation at a secluded cabin in the mountains?"

Dean pushed his plastic fork through his dessert, slipped a slice of the rich, chocolate concoction into his mouth, and met Jo's gaze, which brimmed with undisguised skepticism. Considering she was used to dealing with hardened criminals on the lam, he couldn't blame her for being suspicious and cautious—even if that lack of trust was at his expense. The damning evidence and reports she carried with her about "Dean Colter," coupled with what she'd witnessed back at his house led her to believe he'd been on the verge of eluding authorities.

No matter how personal and private his reasons were for needing the time off, he opted to stick with the truth. Hopefully, when his real identity was revealed in a few days, she'd remember how honest he'd been with her from the moment she'd taken him into custody. Besides, he had no reason to lie.

"I haven't had a real vacation in years and I needed time away from work and life in general to think about an important decision I need to make. So, yes, I suppose on some level stress does come into play." He turned his attention back to his mousse cake for another bite, then continued. "When my father passed away from a heart attack three years ago, the responsibility of Colter Traffic Control became mine, whether I wanted it or not. And every bit of my time and energy since then has been spent making sure the business remained profitable and successful, to the point that I've sacrificed a personal life, among other things.''

"You don't sound like you were too thrilled about taking on the reins of the family business,'' she commented lightly.

Did she believe his story? He searched her carefully composed expression for some kind of sign, found none, and guessed that she was just catering to what she no doubt assumed was a big, elaborate tale. ''I'm not sure how I felt at the time, honestly. After graduating college I went to work at CTC because that's what my father wanted and it seemed like the right thing to do. But I can't say that it would have been the choice I would have made if I hadn't felt pressured into it.''

She leaned back in her chair and crossed her arms over her chest, which drew his gaze to her shapely breasts and the enticing way they pushed against her cotton tank top. ''Why did you feel pressured?''

He ignored the stirring of desire making itself known and finished the last of his cold soda with a loud slurp. In that moment, it dawned on him that he was on the receiving end of a subtle interrogation. She was bombarding him with questions, waiting for him to crack or reveal an inconsistent thread in his story. Hard to do when everything was the bottom-line truth.

"I'm an only child, and spent most of my life listening to my father tell me that the sacrifices he'd made, all the late hours and weekends he spent at work, and all the Little League games and even my high school graduation he'd missed, were all for *me*, because he wanted to make sure he left me with a legacy, unlike his own dad who'd skipped out on him when he was ten and left him and his family with nothing." Unfortunately, that pressure and guilt his father had instilled in him at such an early age had lain heavy on his conscience as an adult.

"So, when Dad died, I had this misguided notion that I had his legacy to carry on. Not only that, but one of the biggest lessons my old man ever taught me was that you don't shirk your responsibilities, and this was a huge obligation for me. There was no other person to take over the business, and my first concern and priority was making sure that my mother was taken care of financially so she wouldn't ever have to worry about money. She received a nice chunk of life insurance that she used to pay off the house they'd bought a few months before Dad's heart failed, but she was also accustomed to the steady income that came in from the business. It was only logical, for so many reasons, that I keep the company and make the best of an unwanted situation."

It was a choice that had caused a whole lot of dissension between him and his fiancée at the time, until Lora finally came to the conclusion one night, when he'd had to cancel dinner plans once again for work, that she couldn't handle being second to a business that was absorbing more and more of his time. Their breakup had been painful and hard on both of them, yet Dean hadn't been able to slow down long enough to make amends. And eventually, he'd found himself sucked into the same vicious cycle that had consumed his father—working late, spending weekends in the office, bidding on every job available and gaining contract after contract until his days and nights became one big blur of paperwork centered around the company.

"All things considered, that was a very selfless choice you made." Her voice was quiet, without the sarcasm he would have expected if she still believed he was trying to deceive her. Despite that small concession, ingrained caution and realistic uncertainties still lingered in the depths of her blue eyes.

"At the time, it was the *only* choice I could make," he told her, stretching his long legs beneath the small table. His calf accidentally brushed hers, and he could have sworn her breath hitched before she scooted back about two feet, moving her own legs out of his reach. "Three years later, things have changed. *I've* changed, and I don't want to make the wrong choice this time out of obligation to anyone but myself."

She digested that, silent and contemplating, staring at him in a way that made him feel as though she was scrutinizing him from the inside out. Her long, slender fingers fluttered against her cheek, then absently pushed wispy strands of hair that had escaped her ponytail away from her face. Which made him envision that thick mass of rich brown hair loose and spread around her shoulders, draped like silk over a pillow, wrapped tight around his long, seeking fingers as he moved over her...

"So," she finally said, bringing him back to the present with a jolt that made him aware that he was undeniably turned on by his private, tantalizing fantasy. "This important decision you claim you need to make, does it have anything to do with your company?"

"As a matter of fact, it does." She was sharp and perceptive, not that he'd expect anything less from her. "A few months ago I received a call from another traffic control company in San Francisco that expressed interest in buying out CTC so they can corner the traffic control market in Seattle, as well. That's why I was heading off for a week in the mountains, to rest, relax, and consider my options and figure out if I want to keep the company because it's all I know, or pursue another unknown career before I'm too old to do so." And regain a personal, social life in the process, he added inwardly.

He stuffed his trash into the paper bag and pitched it into the nearby trash can, enjoying that he could talk so openly with Jo about the issues that had plagued him for months, even if she did doubt his sincerity. "The one thing I do know for certain is that I want to slow down this hectic pace I've been keeping for the past three years, because I don't want to end up having a heart attack like my father. I'd also like a life of my own that doesn't include eighty-hour workweeks. Last month I spent a week in San Francisco with this company hashing out details and legal and monetary issues, and they recently came back with a multimillion-dollar figure I'd be a fool not to at least consider...."

His voice trailed off as a glaring realization struck him hard. He sat there, momentarily stunned, unable to believe he hadn't drawn such an obvious conclusion sooner to explain this entire misunderstanding he'd become a part of.

"I just thought of something," he said, experiencing a bout of frustration that he couldn't stand up when he wanted to pace off the sudden energy buzzing through him. "Something really important that could explain this mess I'm in."

Her gaze narrowed on him, sharp and watchful. "And what's that?"

She was offering him the benefit of any doubts she might harbor about him and his alleged arrest, and he jumped on the opportunity to reveal his theory. "During that last business trip to San Francisco, my briefcase was stolen, which held my wallet and ID—my driver's license, social security card, credit cards. All of it," he said, waving his free hand in the air between them. "The theft happened in the hotel where I was staying, on the day that I was checking out to come home. It was a Friday afternoon, the lobby was packed with guests who were checking in, and I didn't think twice about setting my briefcase down beside me at the registration desk. When I was done with the transaction, my briefcase was gone and nobody in the general vicinity saw anyone take it."

Silent and thoughtful, she chewed on her lush bottom lip, and the slender, jean-clad leg crossed over her opposite knee bounced restlessly. He took her contemplative mood as a sign that she was at least mulling over his story.

He continued on while he still had her full attention, before she decided he was feeding her yet another well-crafted line. "At the time it happened, I thought I was just a victim of a random theft. But after seeing all that stuff you have on file for Dean Colter, including the driver's license that was *stolen,* I'm not so sure."

A slight frown turned down the corners of her mouth. "What, exactly, are you getting at?"

"Jo...someone used my ID to assume my identity," he said, unable to mask the insistence in his tone, or the underlying plea for her to believe him. "Someone who looks *very* similar to me, with dark hair, green eyes and the same features. Except he's a felon, and I'm not. It's the only explanation that makes sense because the guy in that mug shot you have on file sure as hell isn't me."

She stood and cleaned up the remnants of her own dinner, a light, feminine sigh escaping her. "You know, I have to admit I'm finding it very difficult to argue your logic, mainly because I've been on the road for nearly ten hours, and I'm flat-out exhausted and my mind is feeling sluggish. However, even if what you say is true, there's no way to verify your claim on the road. You're going to have to wait until we're back in San Francisco and we can get you fingerprinted." She dumped her empty soda cup into the trash and looked back up at him, meeting his gaze. "I'm really sorry, Dean," she said softly.

He held her stare, his cuffed hand curling into a tight fist beneath the table. "Do *you* believe me, Jo?"

She hesitated for a heartbeat. "I don't know," she said honestly, sounding confused and torn, which gave him a semblance of satisfaction. "Ultimately it doesn't matter what I believe, and I can't let you go based on the evidence I have against you. Besides, in another day we'll both know the truth of who you really are, won't we?"

Resignation wove through him, leaving him no choice but to accept the current circumstances, no matter how helpless they made him feel now that he'd figured out the hows and whys of this false arrest.

Back to Plan B: his seduction and her surrender.

"I take it that means the cuffs stay on until then?"

"For the most part, I'm afraid so." She rubbed her temples, and allowed a tired smile to touch her lips. "I think what I need right now after the long day I've had is a hot shower to clear my head."

"Good idea, though you might want to take me into the bathroom with you while you take a shower," he suggested shamelessly. "Because you just never know what kind of trouble I might get into out here all by myself."

5

Jo left Dean sitting on a chair next to the bed with both hands cuffed to the thick, sturdy headboard post while she ducked into the bathroom, alone and with the door closed, to take her quick shower and change for the evening. He'd feigned a sexy pout when she'd turned down his outrageous request to join her, but had complied without argument when she'd instead secured him to the bed and turned on the TV to a movie channel for him to watch until she returned.

Stepping beneath the pounding spray, she groaned as the water pummeled away the tension in her back and neck and cascaded down the length of her body. Leaving Dean by himself, even for the short period of time she'd be in the shower, was an extension of trust she offered very few of her prisoners. Then again, even from the first moment when she'd surprised him in his garage there had been nothing standard about Dean in terms of criminal behavior or ulterior motives. The man played the role of upstanding citizen very well, his accommodating attitude remaining consistent even in the face of the very dire circumstances awaiting him back in San Francisco. No matter how she sized up Dean Colter, his easygoing actions didn't fit the profile of a felon who was on his way back to jail to face charges of grand theft auto and the possibility of testifying against a powerful ringleader.

Pouring a large dollop of shampoo into her palm, she soaped up her hair and scrubbed her tight scalp as her mind pondered everything he'd revealed during dinner—about his father's death, the company he'd inherited but had strong reservations about truly wanting, and even the robbery of his briefcase, which held all his identification. And try as she might, she hadn't been able to poke holes in his "assumed identity" theory. The incident sounded so realistic and unrehearsed, like he'd truly lived every bit of the story he'd revealed.

Against her better judgment, she was teetering on the precarious cusp of believing him. His thought process was too damned logical and convincing to dismiss as something he'd fabricated on a moment's notice. Those instincts she'd relied on for so many years as a cop urged her to trust him and his revelation. Unfortunately, she had little faith left in those gut intuitions after they'd led her astray with Brian.

Determined not to make another stupid mistake when she was just starting to prove her credibility to Cole again, she decided that while she'd grant Dean Colter a bit of leniency for good behavior, he'd remain in custody until they arrived at their destination and they could clear his name.

Satisfied with her plan, she rinsed her hair and then grabbed the melon-scented shower gel she'd brought with her. She quickly soaped up her body, then washed away the suds with the caress of her hands…down her neck, chest and arms. Her fingers grazed the straining, beaded tips of her nipples on their journey downward, and her pulse picked up its beat as her breasts swelled with excruciating sensitivity.

It had been forever since she'd felt so aware of herself as a woman, even longer since she'd been intimate with a man. Her last long-term relationship had been in college, to be exact, before her profession as a cop became a source of contention for the men she'd dated. They either felt intimidated by her job or wanted to protect her, and both issues always rubbed her the wrong way, to the point that she'd stopped letting anyone get too close. Physically or emotionally.

Since Brian's death, she'd suppressed sensual needs in lieu of pouring her time and energy into solving her abduction cases. But now, her body was screaming for attention, reminding her of baser longings that needed to be attended to, a physical hunger that had grown since she'd been in Dean's presence.

Before she could stop herself, she slowly turned back toward the shower spray and cupped her full, aching breasts in her hands, gently squeezing the soft flesh while the heated water added a more arousing massage. Her thumbs lazily circled the velvety tips of her aureoles, and her breath hitched in her throat at the needy, wanton feeling coiling deep inside her—a demand she'd ignored for far too long. The slow, insistent throb would take very little to appease, she knew. She bit her bottom lip and wondered...if she took the edge off her desire now, maybe, hopefully, she'd no longer lust and fantasize about a man who was incredibly sexy and gorgeous and totally off-limits to her.

Giving in to the urge to let her imagination be a little wild and uninhibited, she allowed her lashes to flutter closed. And that easily, Dean was inside the steamy shower with her, his big hands replacing hers as they gradually skimmed lower, blazing a heated trail down her quivering stomach. With her eyes shut tight and her mind focused on pure pleasure, the silky cascade of water along her skin turned just as seductive as a lover's warm, seeking mouth...as erotic as the slow, sensual lap of an experienced tongue gliding across her belly, licking along her thighs, and burrowing in between, where long, skillful fingers found and stroked the swollen nub of flesh hidden there.

Falling under her own spell, she braced herself against the shower wall, let her head fall back, and surrendered to the provocative fantasy the man in the other room had evoked. She welcomed the swelling, tingling rush of her orgasm building and cresting within her. Her breathing grew heavy in an effort not to moan, her knees buckled, and she finally let go and lost herself in the torrent of sensation flooding her limbs.

Seconds later, she opened her eyes and refocused on her surroundings—alone again, her phantom lover gone. Her heart pounded erratically in her chest and steam from her hot shower billowed around her, as feverish as the climax that she now realized had merely been a temporary solution to obscure her more forbidden desires. Her release had lessened the immediate need that had taken up residence in her, but she still felt empty and unfulfilled in other ways…and she was dismayed to realize her yearning for Dean, the flesh-and-blood man, had only grown stronger.

Refusing to dwell on that revelation, she turned off the water, stepped out of the shower and quickly dried off with a towel. She changed into clean panties, then threw on the cotton shorts and T-shirt she wore to sleep in when she was on a bail recovery assignment. After fastening her leather holster once again to her left side and clipping her keys to the buttonhole in the elastic waistband of her shorts, she brushed her teeth, ran a comb through her damp hair, and dumped all her toiletries back into her cosmetic bag.

All in all, her time in the bathroom had taken less than ten minutes. Gathering her personal items, she opened the door and stepped back into the sleeping area as a warm vapor cloud of moisture followed in her wake. She found Dean right where she'd left him, sitting in what had to be an uncomfortable position in the chair with his hands fastened against the headboard. An action-adventure movie featuring Bruce Willis flickered on the TV screen, but his attention was focused solely on her…which started at her bare legs and gradually worked its way upward.

Eventually his gaze touched on her loose hair, free from the restraint of the ponytail she'd worn earlier, then lingered appreciatively on her freshly scrubbed face, which was flushed, she knew—from his slow perusal, the heated shower she'd taken, and other intimacies she'd indulged in. And just remembering what she'd done with him in her *mind* sent a renewed flash of heat skittering across her skin.

A charming grin slid into place. "You certainly look refreshed."

If he only knew. Holding tight to her composure, she walked to the dresser and dumped her dirty clothes and toiletry bag into her duffle. "A hot shower was just what I needed." In more ways than one.

"Did you leave any hot water for me?" he asked.

"Maybe." She zipped up her bag and turned back to face him. "Depends on what for."

He tipped his head, causing a dark lock of hair to fall across his forehead, which only added to his roguish appeal. "Don't *I* get any bathroom privileges?"

She crossed her arms over her chest and gave his question serious consideration. The bathroom was small and without any windows or other devices that would provide an escape, so she knew he'd be safe and secure in there. She'd give him time for a shower and other personal matters, if he didn't have any qualms about adhering to her rules.

"I suppose receiving bathroom privileges all depends on how modest you are," she told him.

"That depends on how modest *you* are," he countered right back, without an ounce of reserve or bashfulness fringing his deep, rich voice.

Undeniable amusement curled through her as she strolled toward him and stopped a foot away. "I've just about seen it all during my time as a cop, and trust me when I say that modesty has no place on the job." For all her frankness and direct words, she had a strong feeling seeing Dean buck naked would test her professional indifference, especially since he'd just starred in her own private fantasy.

Tapping into a humorous incident from her patrol days, she shared it with him. "There was one time my partner and I chased a suspect over the walls of a nudist colony, which put me up close and personal with every shape, size, and color of anatomy available to the human race. The experience was quite an eye-opener, so I doubt you have something I haven't already seen before."

"Ouch." He feigned an affronted wince, though the mischievous light shining in his eyes gave him away. "You sure know how to deflate a guy's ego."

Unable to help herself, she laughed lightly. "Let's put it this way. If you don't mind an audience, you're welcome to use the bathroom...with certain restrictions, of course."

"Of course." He heaved an inflated sigh. "Lay 'em on me, sweetheart."

"I'll take off your handcuffs so you can use the bathroom freely, but you'll strip down to your briefs out here—"

"What if I don't wear any?" he interrupted, clearly looking to rattle her with the possibility.

She remained outwardly unruffled and called his

bluff with a nonchalant shrug of her shoulder. "Then you strip down to the buff."

He grinned devilishly. "Just checking."

Which didn't answer the question of whether or not he wore any underwear beneath his jeans. She swallowed hard. "I'll get whatever clothes you want to wear and any toiletries you need from your duffle, and you'll have five minutes in the shower."

"Hey, you took longer than that," he protested.

The flush on her skin deepened when she recalled how she'd spent those extra minutes. "That's one of the perks of being in charge." She tossed him a tough-luck kind of look and stood her ground. "Five minutes, take it or leave it, Mr. Colter."

He shifted in his chair, and the cuffs rattled against the hard wood post. "I'll take it."

"And you'll leave the door open about a foot at all times," she went on, laying down more restrictions. He opened his mouth to say something, and she held up a hand to cut him off. "My rules aren't negotiable. I'm willing to give you a bit of freedom, with your *full* cooperation. Again, one false move and—"

"I'll be flat on my ass and trussed up for the duration of the ride home," he finished for her.

This time, *she* grinned. "Nice to know we're on the same wavelength."

"You drive a hard bargain, Jo."

She grew serious, wanting him to know that he was, indeed, getting a bargain when it came to his request to take a shower. "I've given you more fringe benefits than I usually give any person I've taken into custody.'' She turned away before he could question her generosity and the trust she was extending on his behalf. She might have her doubts about him being the man the police sought, but she wasn't about to let *him* know that.

She returned to the dresser. ''Now, what would you like from your duffle bag?''

''There's a pair of gray cotton sweatpants in there,'' he said from behind her. ''I'll sleep in those.''

She opened the canvas bag and retrieved the article of clothing he'd mentioned, then glanced over her shoulder and forced herself to ask, ''How about underwear?''

He shook his head, the barest hint of a disarming smile curving his lips. ''Too binding to sleep in.''

Too binding to wear during the day, as well? she wondered. She'd find out soon enough. ''How about a T-shirt?''

''No, thanks. I'm wearing the sweatpants purely out of courtesy. I don't usually wear anything at all to bed.''

Oh, boy. Cool sheets rustling against hot, bare skin flitted through her mind, a tempting, erotic vision she quickly banished. ''Anything else that you want or need?''

His eyes held hers, and the subdued lighting cast from the lamp between the two beds turned his irises a deep, golden-green hue. ''There's a whole lot that I want and need, Jo,'' he murmured huskily, ''but for now I'll settle for my shaving kit.''

A shiver rippled down her spine and caused her already sensitized breasts to swell with awareness. Inhaling a breath, she pulled out the leather toiletry bag and rummaged through the contents for anything that could be used as a weapon, and found nothing more dangerous than a razor to shave with. "Shampoo, soap and deodorant only," she said, confiscating the sharped-edged instrument. "Sorry, no razors allowed."

"Then that's all I need." He blinked lazily, and added, "For now."

She put his sweatpants and the few toiletries she'd approved into the bathroom, then returned to release him. Sitting on the edge of the mattress near him, but careful to keep her revolver out of direct reaching distance, she unclipped her set of keys and leaned over to unlock the metal restraints shackling his hands—doing her best to dismiss the hot feel of his skin beneath her fingertips as she worked to unbind him.

Once he was free, he slowly stood and rubbed his wrists while she fastened the cuffs along the top strap of her shoulder holster to use when he was done with his shower. Remaining seated on the bed, she motioned him in the middle of the room in front of her. "Go ahead and turn around, face the wall, and get undressed." It was the only bit of privacy she'd allow.

He did as she ordered. Watching him was merely a safety tactic, she told herself as he pulled his T-shirt from the waistband of his jeans and revealed an enticing strip of smooth flesh around his torso. A precautionary measure to ensure there was nothing lethal hidden on his person before he walked into the bathroom, she lectured herself as he worked the cotton material up and over his head and she stared in pure female fascination at the intriguing way the muscles bisecting his back pulled and stretched with the movement.

Except safety and precaution had little to do with the pulsing knot of desire that once again formed in her stomach—a sensation that was much too pleasurable and not at all professional. Then again, taking into consideration the slow, purposeful way he was stripping, she had to wonder if he was deliberately attempting to tease her senses.

If so, he was doing a damned good job.

He dropped the shirt to the floor and toed off his shoes, then pulled off his socks, and again she was treated to another round of muscles rippling, in his arms and across his shoulders.

The sound of metal scraping against metal sounded much too erotic in the quiet room as he unzipped his pants. He tucked his thumbs into the waistband, and she held her breath as he inched the denim downward, and exhaled gratefully when he remained clad in a pair of white briefs that hugged his tight posterior.

Then, without warning, he turned around, and she found herself staring at the juncture of his muscular thighs. Her cheeks flamed when she realized that he was semi-aroused, too. Her gaze shot up to his, and he grinned unapologetically.

"Do I pass inspection?" The double entendre in his voice and coating his words was unmistakable.

Just so long as the only concealed weapon on you isn't loaded. The saucy reply zipped through her mind but, thankfully, didn't escape her mouth.

Clearing her throat, she smoothed damp strands of hair behind her ear. "You pass just fine. Five minutes in the shower," she reminded him, then glanced at her wristwatch, surprised to discover it was already a quarter after eight. "I'll let you know when your time is up."

"Then I'd better get started and not waste any of my time." With a playful wink, he turned and entered the bathroom, leaving the door cracked open a good twelve inches as she'd requested. Seconds later the rush of water echoed into the outer room, and the click of the shower door indicated he'd stepped inside the stall.

She leaned to the left a few inches just to verify that he was, indeed, inside the shower and caught a glimpse of bare skin, and so much more than she'd intended. Even though the glass enclosure was frosted, she could still define his silhouette and identify features—like his broad chest that tapered into a lean torso and gave way to athletic thighs.

A warm, sexual glow spread through her. The man was so completely, overwhelmingly masculine, in every way possible. And despite what she'd said earlier about doubting he had something she hadn't already seen before, she was forced now to admit that she'd been wrong. Very, very wrong. He was amply, generously endowed. Impressively so.

A groan escaped her throat. Good Lord, if she didn't turn her mind to something else, like business, she'd end up ogling Dean throughout his entire shower. Not an unpleasant thought at all, if the circumstances between them were different. But, according to her file, he was a man wanted by the law for a crime he'd yet to face trial for.

Or was he?

With that perplexing question weighing heavily on her mind, she slipped off the bed and retrieved the file on Dean that she'd brought in from the truck, determined to find more clear-cut answers. She skimmed through the paperwork once again, searching for a shred of proof that might corroborate the story he'd told her earlier. Unfortunately, all she discovered in the formal documents and police reports was glaring evidence against him.

She chewed absently on her bottom lip while broadening her way of thinking. If someone *had* assumed his identity, then of course all those physical statistics and the personal identification of the man who'd stolen his ID would match with Dean's, as they did in the paperwork filed by the police. And if he had been robbed of his wallet, then there would be undeniable facts to validate that particular claim.

With that in mind, she went back to Dean's duffle bag and rechecked the driver's license in a leather billfold that hadn't yet been broken in. Sure enough, the issue date beneath his photo was only a few weeks ago. She rummaged further and found credit cards that appeared to be brand new, then withdrew a stash of about a dozen business cards that were tucked into one of the compartments of the wallet and read the navy blue imprint: Colter Traffic Control, Dean Colter, President.

"I'll be damned," she muttered, her head spinning with the knowledge that Dean's story, for the most part, seemed credible. Everything she'd just discovered lent credence to his claim of innocence, yet without fingerprints to establish his true identity, she couldn't set him free and risk the very slim possibility that her gut intuition might be wrong.

"Did I beat the clock, warden?"

Startled by Dean's deep voice so near, she let his wallet slip through her fingers and drop to the floor, and she spun back around as a surge of adrenaline rushed through her blood. Her hand automatically reached for the beanbag shotgun that wasn't attached to her waistband, but lay on the bed between them where she'd left it after her shower.

Shit. With no other option available, she gripped the handle of her revolver. Her stomach pitched, and she knew if he stepped any closer and posed any threat to her at all this was where her black belt in martial arts would come in handy, because she knew she wouldn't be able to remove her weapon from her holster with the intent of using it on him.

Frustration and anger swept through her at her weakness, and the fact that she'd let down her guard when she knew better. What the hell had she been thinking?

She shored up her mental and physical defenses. "Don't move," she warned.

He stood absolutely still, his hair damp and tousled around his head, and wearing nothing but his gray cotton sweatpants. Slowly, he held up both hands with fingers spread wide in a gesture of acquiescence. "Whoa, Jo, I'm sorry," he said, instantly contrite, his gaze on the revolver she'd yet to withdraw. "I swear I didn't mean to startle you. I thought you heard me get out of the shower."

Her jaw clenched, and she was loath to admit that she'd been so caught up in her search for his innocence he'd taken her completely by surprise. Stupid, stupid, stupid!

When she issued no response, he nodded toward the shower. "Do you want me to get my personal things out of the bathroom for you?"

She shook her head, and unable to detect any signs of danger from him, she finally let her hand fall away from her weapon, but remained physically alert. "No, *I'll* do it." A thread of irritation underscored her tone—not directed at him, but at her own foolishness for putting herself in such a vulnerable position when she knew the consequences that could result from being too relaxed, too trusting. And claiming extreme exhaustion and being caught up in doubts about this man's criminal charges were no excuse for being careless and leaving herself so exposed.

"Then I guess this is the end of my freedom for

now, huh?'' He held his wrists in front of him, offering himself back into her custody.

"'Fraid so,'' she said evenly, despite how shaken she still was by the incident and what could have happened with someone more vindictive. Keeping her gaze on him, she quickly stooped down to retrieve the wallet she'd dropped and stuffed it back into his bag, then approached him cautiously, regaining control of herself and the situation.

She snapped one of the silver loops around his right wrist, and made sure that the far side of his bed was away from anything he could use to his advantage, or against her. "I'm going to have to cuff at least one of your hands to the headboard during the night,'' she told him.

"I figured as much.'' He grinned indulgently and sat down on the edge of the mattress, making it incredibly easy for her to fasten the other cuff to the post without so much as a protest from him. "Besides, it all ties into that captive and bondage fantasy I'm trying to indulge in.''

"Whatever turns you on,'' she said without thinking, then realized the double entendre when their eyes met and the wicked gleam in the depths of his told her that *she* turned him on.

A now familiar frisson of awareness took up residence, and she did the smart thing and moved away. He settled onto the bed, making himself as comfortable as possible considering how limited he was with one arm shackled to the headboard. With his free hand tucked beneath the pillow behind his head, and his gorgeous, long, lean body sprawled the length of the mattress, he appeared content and relaxed as he watched the television in front of him.

She inhaled a calming breath. Damn him, anyway—for being so cooperative and accommodating, and for making her harbor doubts and uncertainties that had no business taking up residence within her.

Turning away, she dragged her fingers through her damp hair. She needed sleep. At least eight solid hours of it if she expected to make the long drive back to Oakland tomorrow in one straight shot and with a clear head. She cleaned up the bathroom, leaving the light on and the door cracked to provide a shaft of illumination into the room throughout the night, then stuffed the clothes he'd stripped out of into his duffle and set her travel alarm clock for six o'clock. After taking off her shoulder holster, she stowed her gun beneath the pillow on the far side of her bed for safekeeping and double-checked to make sure her keys were still attached to her waistband— all the while ignoring the heat of Dean's stare as he watched her.

"Mind handing me the remote?" he asked pleasantly, just as she pulled down the covers to climb into her bed.

"Keep the volume down and turn off the TV when you get tired." She tossed him the gadget, and in typical male fashion he immediately channel-surfed in search of a program that interested him. She turned off the lamp on the nightstand separating their beds, throwing the room into shifting shadows from the glow of the TV, then slipped between her cool, clean sheets.

"Good night, Jo," he said, his low, intimate voice reaching to her side of the room. "Sweet dreams."

Sweet, erotic dreams of him, he'd no doubt meant. "Yeah, you, too," she muttered.

He chuckled warmly. "Now *that* sounded sincere."

She *refused* to smile. Refused to enjoy his attempt at humor when she was so conflicted about him, about her reaction to his mere presence, and about the need to believe he was as innocent as he claimed.

Punching her pillow to fluff it, she curled up on her side facing the opposite direction of him, but couldn't succumb to the weariness pulling at her subconscious. After the day she'd had and the events of the last hour, it took her body longer than she'd expected to wind down. She didn't completely relax until Dean shut off the TV a good hour later and she finally heard his breathing grow deep and even in slumber.

Then, and only then, did she let herself drift off to sleep.

6

blaze of the TV, the reflections wavering across her cheeks.

"Jo," he attempted in a low voice, his frustration mounting as he realized he couldn't touch her. "Jo, wake up, baby."

"No!" she cried, the sound anguished.

"Jo," he said, more firmly, "Jo, sweetheart—"

DEAN WOKE UP in the middle of the night to the disturbing sound of frightened whimpers, and Jo thrashing frantically in the bed next to his. He'd wished her sweet dreams, but it seemed nightmares were plaguing her instead.

The bathroom light Jo had left on supplied enough illumination for him to see her tossing and turning restlessly beneath the sheets twisted around her legs. "No, please don't leave me," she moaned, and her breath caught on a soul-deep sob as she kicked even harder to free herself from the restricting covers. "You *can't* die. You can't. I won't let you!"

She sounded so terrified, and his heart gave a funny twist in his chest at the too-real despair and anguish in her voice. Wanting to soothe her and chase away whatever demons overpowered her mind, he attempted to move across the expanse of bed separating them, and cursed vividly when he was brought up short by the arm cuffed to the headboard.

"It's all my fault," she groaned raggedly, openly crying now, the stream of tears slipping down the sides of her face glittering like quicksilver from the light. "I'm sorry...so sorry," she chanted as she wept, her pain a tangible thing.

Annoyed at his inability to reach her and wake her from the throes of her bad dream, Dean used the only resource available to him. His voice. *"Jo,"* he called, loud and firm enough to snap her out of her sleep-induced nightmare.

She sat up abruptly in bed, her chest heaving and fingers clutching the blankets in her lap. Her unfocused gaze darted around the room, taking in her surroundings, trying to latch onto something familiar. She shook her head, looking completely lost and disoriented.

"Sweetheart," he murmured gently, not wanting to frighten her any more than she already was. "Are you okay?"

A frown creased her brows, and she slowly glanced toward him as her hands absently shoved her disheveled hair from her face. She tipped her head in his direction. "Brian?" she asked softly, confusion and hope mingling in her quivering voice.

He had no idea who this Brian person was. He didn't think it was a husband or boyfriend since she'd denied having either, but judging by her glazed eyes and perplexed expression, he guessed she was still asleep, her subconscious still submerged in a hypnoticlike trance. He decided to play along, just to keep her calm and subdue her angst and distress. No doubt she'd fall right back to sleep and wouldn't remember any of this in the morning, which was just as well, considering how bizarre the whole entire incident seemed.

"Yeah, it's me," he said, keeping his response vague and letting her come to her own conclusions in her mind about who he was. "And you're fine, Jo."

A shudder of relief shook her shoulders. "You're not really dead."

Her gratitude wrapped around him like a physical and emotional cloak, making him a part of whatever torment lived deep within her soul. Her heartache was authentic and sincere and obviously intertwined with the desperate need to believe that this Brian person was still alive. That *he* was still alive.

Swallowing the tight knot in his throat, he granted her wish. "No, I'm not dead."

Instead of lying down and falling back to sleep as he'd expected her to do, she tugged at the blankets around her legs and finally managed to untangle the covers from her long limbs. Slipping from her bed, she approached his, and Dean held his breath and remained completely still, uncertain what she intended.

Without hesitation, and with too much trust, she crawled across the mattress and snuggled up to his side, oblivious to his other hand cuffed to the post. Oblivious, too, to the fact that she was as defenseless and susceptible as a person could get—and embracing a man she believed, in her conscious state, was a felon.

Oh, hell. He'd kicked off his own covers long ago, and her head came to rest on his shoulder. She pressed her slender hand to his bare chest, right over his rapidly beating heart, and at her gentle, evocative touch, it picked up its pace.

So did his libido.

He bit back a deep groan as she stroked her hand down his stomach and nuzzled her face against his neck. "I thought..." The entire length of her shuddered before she continued, "Oh, God, I thought he killed you," she whispered in a raw tone of voice. "And I couldn't bring myself to shoot back and I couldn't move and you were lying there, dying, and I felt so helpless...."

She was babbling, her mind caught up in a scenario too gruesome for him to comprehend, and the last thing he wanted was for her to turn hysterical on him. Experiencing a surge of possessiveness that took him momentarily off guard, he turned his head and brushed his warm lips against her temple. He inhaled the delicate melon scent that clung to her skin, which instigated a fresh rush of tenderness to well up in him.

"Shhh," he coaxed, and with a little maneuvering he managed to slide his free arm around her shoulders to pull her close, into the safety of his embrace. "It's okay, Jo. We're both fine," he assured her.

"Yes, you're fine," she murmured drowsily. Wrapping her arm around his middle, she nestled her body tight against his. One of her knees slipped between his legs, and he tried not to think about the intimacy of their position. Or how mortified she was going to be when she discovered what she'd done in the middle of the night.

"It was all a bad, horrible dream," she mumbled, her words slow and lethargic.

"Yeah, a bad dream," he agreed, though from her vivid reaction, he suspected that reality had played some part in creating the terrifying images that had afflicted her mind. And who, he wondered, was Brian? And was the other man alive or dead?

He pondered the possibilities as he threaded her silky soft hair through his fingers and gently massaged her scalp to lull her back to sleep and, he hoped, to sweeter dreams. His ploy worked. She sighed contentedly, her mint-scented breath fanning evenly across his throat, leaving his skin moist and hot and excruciatingly sensitive. After a few minutes of pampering, her body relaxed completely and leaned heavily against him as she dozed off again. The ultrasoft, feminine curves of her waist, hips and thighs branded him, and her even softer, lush breasts crushed too provocatively against his chest.

That quickly he grew hard and thick and fiercely aroused, and there wasn't anything he could do to curb his deprived body's instinctively male response to her cuddling and warm female scent. He'd be damn lucky to get any more rest tonight when all he could think about was how much he wanted this seemingly tough, in-control female bounty hunter who was sexier and sassier than any woman he'd had the enjoyment of tangling with in a long, long time. A woman who possessed a vulnerable side that drew him and made him want to discover all her deep, dark secrets.

Despite the evidence against Dean Colter she carried in her file, there was a mutual attraction they'd be hard-pressed to deny if confronted head-on with the shared fascination. He'd seen the desire in her eyes when he'd stripped off his clothes earlier, could feel the sensuality shimmering between them.

She was fighting temptation, struggling valiantly against the promise of pleasure that beckoned and teased them both. And she would continue to do so until he proved his innocence, he thought with a frustrated sigh.

She inhaled a deep, peaceful breath, exhaled slowly, and the set of keys fastened to the waistband of her shorts slipped lower and scraped along his belly. They taunted him, daring him to take advantage of his one chance to validate Jo's doubts about his criminal status and demonstrate how trustworthy he truly was.

A slow, sly smile formed. It was time for the captor to become the captured. And in the process, they'd finally put to the test the attraction they'd both been skirting since she'd cornered him in his garage and frisked him.

WITH A LOW GROAN, Jo stretched her aching muscles and tried to roll to her side, certain her alarm clock would chime at any second to wake her up. Her right arm refused to follow the movement of the rest of her body, and instead ended up twisted at an awkward angle above her head. Frowning at the odd sensation biting around her wrist, and perplexed at the unexplainable and uncomfortable position she seemed to be in, she blinked her lashes open and found herself looking directly at her prisoner reclining casually on *her* bed, his head propped up by his hand, unrestrained and completely in control.

He stared at her in return, the dark stubble lining his lean jaw intensifying the green hue of his eyes. "Good morning, sweetheart," he drawled in greeting.

She barely heard his words...not when her mind filled immediately with alarm that he'd managed to escape somehow. Then pure, undiluted panic registered when she yanked on her hand again and realized *she* was the one secured to the headboard of the bed, putting her at his mercy. Adding to her internal chaos was the knowledge that her keys and revolver were on the nightstand between them...far, far out of reaching distance.

Her heart beat so hard she feared it would explode from her chest. She had no idea how she'd gotten in this predicament, couldn't remember anything at all to give her a clue as to why she was the one shackled to Dean's bedpost, or how the authority had shifted in Dean's favor.

No matter the hows or whys, she refused to be a victim. She scrambled to a sitting position, preferring to be defensive instead of defenseless. Narrowing her gaze on him, she jutted her chin out. "How did you manage this clever trick?" she asked, opting for a sharp, snide tone to drown out the fear churning in her belly.

He had the audacity to wink at her. "I've always heard a magician never reveals his tricks."

"You're a felon, not a magician," she snapped irritably, hating that this man had somehow, some way, duped her.

He feigned a wince at her well-placed barb, which did nothing to hide the humor dancing in the depth of his eyes. "Come on, Jo," he said, cajoling her with his rich voice and sexy smile. "If I was really a felon on the run, fearful of standing trial back in San Francisco, I would have been long gone by now, leaving you to your own devices and letting the motel maid find you shackled to the bed. And if I was some kind of malicious criminal, I would have taken advantage of you hours ago."

Her heart rate slowed as she mulled over his comment, knowing instinctively that what he said was true—no real convict would have wasted such a prime opportunity to flee. Knowing, too, that his behavior since she'd captured him and the evidence she'd discovered in his wallet all lent undeniable credibility to his innocence. Now she was forced to trust him, his story, and her own intuition.

Believing him came much easier this morning than it had last night, not that she was going to admit that out loud and give him any more leverage than he'd already managed to gain.

Calmer now, she wanted, *needed,* an explanation. "Could you tell me how I ended up cuffed to your bed?" she asked, then followed that up with a polite, "please?"

He grinned at her courteous request. "You had a bad dream last night that had you pretty upset. I called your name to wake you up and you sat up in bed, but you were actually still asleep. You thought I was Brian, and you crawled right across my bed and curled up next to me.''

Disbelief rushed over her, flushing her cheeks with a stinging heat. Her mouth opened to deny his story, then snapped shut again when she realized there was no possible way Dean could have known about Brian...unless she had mentioned his name at some point. And how much had she revealed about her partner and how responsible she'd been for his death?

Appalled that she'd been so bold and brazen as to cuddle up to Dean, especially in her sleep when a person was at their most vulnerable, she flopped back down on the bed and slung her free arm over her eyes and let a low, embarrassed groan escape her.

Bits and pieces of the same old recurring dream filtered through her mind, the same one that terrified and haunted her when she least expected her personal demon to rear its ugly head. Sometimes she recalled the dream the following morning. Other times she woke up in a cold sweat or physically shaking from the vivid images. Often she remembered nothing.

She never knew she talked in her sleep, or worse, walked in her sleep...but she had, right into another man's arms. A man she'd picked up on a criminal charge. A scary, staggering thought, considering all the scenarios that could have happened with someone less sincere and honorable than the true Dean Colter was turning out to be.

She moved her arm up to her forehead to look at

him. "Go on," she urged. "How did you manage the Houdini trick with the cuffs?"

"Your keys were on the waistband of your shorts, within reaching distance of my free hand," he explained with a nonchalant shrug. "And considering the prime opportunity that presented itself, I couldn't resist switching our roles."

She lifted a brow. "Turnabout is fair play for you, huh?" she asked with a reluctant smile at his audacity, even as she recognized that this scenario could have ended up with a much different conclusion in the hands of a true criminal. But there was nothing malicious in Dean's plan, just a playful role reversal he seemed to be enjoying.

And, surprisingly, now that any immediate threat had been eliminated, she found she was enjoying it too.

He blinked lazily. "In our case, turnabout is most definitely fair play, especially when it comes to indulging in fantasies."

An unexpected thrill coursed through her, eliciting a sensual heat that spread to feminine nerve endings. "And what fantasy is that?" she dared to ask.

He splayed his long fingers on the mattress in front of him and grinned roguishly. "*Me* captor, *you* prisoner, with a little bondage thrown in for good measure."

The pulse in her throat fluttered. "There's just one thing you're missing, *Master*."

Amusement flickered across his expression. "And what's that?"

"A submissive female," she replied impudently.

He chuckled, the deep, rich sound making her toes curl and her body warm with awareness. "Oh, I'm not worried about your surrender," he said too confidently. "While I've never done this kind of thing before, I'm a strong believer in the power of persuasion. Especially when it's between two people who are highly attracted to each other."

He'd brought the forbidden out into the open, and she swallowed hard, unable to deny his claim. She'd been battling her attraction to him since yesterday afternoon, had even made him a part of her own personal fantasy last night in the shower. The dynamics of their relationship had shifted this morning to one full of sensual possibilities, and she wondered how far he planned to take things. And just how far she'd allow herself to follow.

Growing suddenly serious, he rolled to a sitting position on the edge of the bed across from hers and braced his arms on either side of his thighs. The tight muscles across his abdomen rippled, drawing her traitorous gaze to the fascinating sight and the thatch of hair that swirled around his navel then disappeared into the waistband of his sweatpants.

"You know," he said, his tone low and gruff, "I hate to be the one to point this out, but you really put yourself in an incredibly dangerous position last night."

She reluctantly lifted her gaze upward, startled to see the concern and caring in the dark depth of his eyes. "No lecture, please. I'm already feeling foolish enough about all this without being reprimanded by my own prisoner, and that's who you are, despite who's currently wearing the handcuffs.'' And if her brothers ever found out about what had happened, she'd be restricted to a desk for the rest of her P.I. days, which wasn't an option for her.

He dragged a hand through his thick, tousled hair. ''I just think you need to be more careful in the future, or else you might end up in the *wrong* guy's bed.'' A teasing note threaded his voice, and he gave her one of his flirtatious winks, lightening the moment. ''This time, you got lucky.''

And ended up in the right guy's bed. *His* bed. And now she was currently secured to said bed and feeling at a distinct disadvantage, regardless of the sexual byplay they'd indulged in minutes ago.

She rattled the metal shackles to bring his attention back to her current position and smiled sweetly for effect. ''You can release me any time.''

He stroked his dark, stubbled chin with his fingers, considering the situation. Considering her. ''Not just yet,'' he decided.

She frowned, annoyance mingling with a restless feeling of arousal. ''I think you made your point by cuffing me to the bedpost.''

He cocked his head. ''Did I?'' he asked, the simple question holding a wealth of doubts.

''Didn't you?'' she shot back just as quickly, ignoring the skip of her pulse, and the tingling sensation skittering down her spine.

He thought for another long, drawn-out moment.

"I'm not sure I made my point yet." In one fluid motion he stood and grabbed her set of keys, then moved across her bed like a big, lithe panther stalking his prey—all powerful, potent magnetism and intoxicating masculinity.

Shameless desire took up residence in her, and intensified when he leaned over her to work the lock on the cuffs. His sweatpants rode low on his hips, and his flat belly was inches away from her face. The musky, all-male scent of him teased her senses, awakening a reckless hunger to do things to him that shocked even herself...like flick her tongue across his warm, hair-roughened flesh to see what he tasted like, or sink her teeth into the soft skin just below his ribs to test how sensitive he might be, or press her lips to the kidney-shaped birthmark on the left side of his navel...

Her breathing deepened, and she squeezed her eyes shut, which did little to block those erotic images she'd conjured, or lessen the temptation he presented when he surrounded her so completely.

"Mind giving me a little help with these cuffs?" he asked from above her.

Grateful for the distraction, she reached up to assist him, but couldn't glance up without risking the possibility of licking, biting or kissing his belly, so she kept her eyes closed. Blindly, she searched for the keys, only to have Dean gently grasp her wrist and snap the other cuff around her free hand, effectively and efficiently restraining her arms above her head.

Her eyes opened wide in astonishment. She jerked

on her restraints, but the effort was futile. The sturdy bedpost wasn't going to budge, break, or pull apart, as she already knew. Dean grinned down at her, but she wasn't amused that he'd managed to dupe her once again. This time while she was wide awake.

"What are you doing?" she demanded.

He settled himself along her left side, singeing her with the scorching heat of his body crowding against her. He pressed his fingers against her lips to hush her, and his striking green eyes met and held hers. "I'm buying a little extra time to find out if I made my point or not," he told her, and slowly let his fingers drift from her mouth, along her jaw, and down the column of her throat. "Do you believe the story I told you last night, about the possibility of someone assuming my identity?"

"You're going to interrogate me?" she asked incredulously.

"For starters," he drawled, and let her overactive imagination come to its own conclusions as to what would come *after* he had the information and answers sought. "Do you believe it's possible that someone assumed my identity?"

She couldn't lie, not when she'd seen so much evidence to back up his claim. "Yes, I do."

Stark relief eased across his chiseled features. "Do you trust me?"

She rolled her eyes and pulled on her bound arms, doing her best to ignore that her T-shirt had ridden up a few inches and exposed too much bare skin.

"Gee, considering my current predicament, I guess I'm going to have to."

"Uh-uh. Not a good enough answer." He shook his head and twirled a section of her hair around his long finger and gave it a playful tug. "I don't want there to be any doubts in your mind about me, Jo. None whatsoever." A slight, concerned frown formed between his brows. "Are you afraid I'm going to hurt you in any way?"

She didn't fear him, but rather her own sexual response to him. Never had she been so attuned to a man as she was to Dean. Never could she remember wanting a man as much as she was beginning to crave him.

"No," she whispered, wondering what that admission would eventually cost her. Nothing she didn't already want to give him, she was certain.

"Good. Because you're perfectly safe with me, in every way," he promised.

She believed him. More than was prudent. More than was wise. In ways she'd never trusted another man, because Dean was straightforward and honest in his actions. He didn't coddle and treat her like a helpless female in need of a man's protection. And despite his dominant position at the moment, despite the provocative game he was playing, she felt safe with him. Was confident that if she called his intentions to a halt this very second, he'd back off and release her.

It was her own willingness that made her his captive, and her own enthusiasm that made her too eager to experience the kind of pleasure she'd denied herself for so long. Too long.

"So," he murmured, tickling the side of her neck with long sweeps of her hair against her skin, causing gooseflesh to rise and her breasts to tingle. "If you're not afraid of me, you must trust me more than you realize or want to admit out loud."

The man was way too smart. Way too intuitive. Verbalizing that trust would break down any last barriers between them and leave her open to all kinds of tantalizing scenarios. She wasn't ready to give him that power over her. Yet. "You're very analytical."

"Just trying to read all the signs accurately, especially when you're being vague with your answers and skirting the issue."

The silence grew as he waited patiently for her answer. Finally, she released a sigh and gave it to him, not out of obligation, but he deserved to know what she thought of him. "I trust you."

An indulgent smile curved his full lips. "Now why do I get the impression that trust is a very hesitant one?"

It wasn't. Not really. But playing hard to get, just a little bit, was better than relinquishing everything up front. "Vivid imagination?" she suggested with a bit of sass.

His irises darkened with smoky desire, and when he shifted one of his rock-hard thighs over hers, she felt the rigid length of his erection pressing against her hip. A throbbing, luxurious ache settled in her stomach, and lower, and she swallowed back the groan rising in her throat.

"Oh, I most definitely have a vivid imagination, Ms. Sommers," he said, having proven as much with his body's lustful response to her. "Especially when it comes to you and me. And us. Together."

She touched her tongue to her upper lip, feeling her entire body hum with anticipation. "Us?"

"Uh-huh," he said, nodding slowly, and let his gaze lower to her mouth. "Tell me, Jo, do you trust me enough to let me kiss you while you're completely at my mercy like this?"

The wanting and excitement increased, coiling tighter within her. She laughed, the sound more nervous than the frivolous note she'd been striving for. Yeah, she was uncertain...of where a kiss with him could lead...of where she yearned for it to lead. "What makes you think I *want* you to kiss me?"

He propped his palm against his temple. His face was inches from hers, nearly within kissing distance. "Oh, just an educated guess."

The sensual secrets glimmering in his eyes, mixed in with the presumptuousness infusing his voice made her too curious. "Based on?"

"The way your breath catches when I touch you."

He followed up that matter-of-fact statement by splaying his large hand on the strip of flesh between the hem of her T-shirt and the elastic waistband of her shorts, and she inhaled quickly at the incendiary heat that rippled through her.

"Yeah, just like that," he said, dark satisfaction

etching his bold, masculine features, along with a good dose of gratification at the impulsive, brazen way she strained toward him.

"And then there's the way your skin quivers with the lightest caress of my fingers," he went on, toying and swirling his pinkie around her sensitive navel until she gasped and squirmed and trembled.

"But the most telling fact that you want me as much as I want you is the way your nipples are growing tight and hard right this second, and the way you're trying to shift closer, for a more intimate contact, a more explicit touch." The tips of his fingers skimmed upward, disappearing beneath her shirt to brush along the full undersides of her breasts, a teasing stroke that left her wanting so much more. "Every one of your responses is a dead giveaway."

He was right. Her responses were uninhibited and wanton, and she couldn't help herself. Arguing his claim was impossible and ridiculous, so she didn't even try, especially when the evidence he'd compiled against her was irrefutable.

His gaze burned into hers, and it was obvious he was holding his own desires for her in check. "You never answered my question, Jo, and a simple yes or no reply will suffice. Do you trust me to kiss you while you're handcuffed to the bed, without having any control over what happens?"

A frightening thought, if the circumstances were different, with a man she *didn't* trust. He might be the one holding the reins of this seduction, but she also recognized that he was giving her the ultimate power right now—to say no, or take a huge leap of faith. With him.

The forbidden beckoned. So did the fantasy of playing hostage to a man who'd master her with his lips, his mouth, his hands. The thought thrilled her, enticed her, aroused her.

"Yes," she breathed.

7

As soon as Dean gained the permission he sought, he tangled his fingers through the silky warmth of her hair at the nape of her neck and tipped her chin up with his thumb beneath her jaw. Lowering his head, he ended the wait, wanting more than his next breath to kiss Jo, to finally taste the desire she exuded. To see if all the sexual tension between them was merely a prelude to a deeper kind of ecstasy.

His mouth settled on hers, sliding slowly, insistently, hotly over hers. Her lips were plush and warm and pliant. Generous. Opening for him and allowing him inside with a soft moan of surrender. With a surge of heat coursing through his veins he exerted a deeper pressure and found her tongue with his. He teased her mercilessly, flirted playfully, and swept the velvet depths of her mouth with seductive forays that coaxed her to be just as bold and daring in return.

She matched his kiss with equal fervor, impetuously chasing his mouth with her own and giving as good as he gave, which heightened his own excitement and inflamed him beyond rational thought or reason. She wasn't shy about indulging in the erotic pleasures of two people who were highly attracted to each other. Wasn't modest about enjoying what felt good. Wasn't at all hesitant in communicating with her lips and tongue and the sinuous movements of her body what she liked and what she wanted more of.

And what she craved was more of *him*.

She couldn't use her hands, couldn't utter a word with her busy, seeking mouth, but she spoke volumes with expressive feminine signals as old as time—a silent, ancient language spoken by a woman to a man, and one he instinctively recognized. The twisting to get closer. The subtle rocking of her hips. The restless shifting of her slender thighs against the one he'd wedged between her legs.

She wanted to be touched, caressed, stroked. Physically and intimately. Wasting no time in fulfilling her need, he glided the hand resting on her waist up her back and smoothed his palm along her spine. She groaned into his mouth and arched and shivered beneath him. Yielding to her body's silent invocation, he flattened his broad hand on the small of her back and pulled her more fully against him, as close as her manacled arms would allow. He nearly came apart when her stiff nipples thrust enticingly against his chest and she entwined her legs tighter around his and squeezed.

His breath hitched as a fierce rush of carnal lust and excruciating need flooded his limbs—the need to do things to and with Jo to extinguish the heat simmering in his gut. He was granite-hard and thicker than he could ever remember being, and more alive than he'd felt in years. All because of this vibrant, sensual woman who'd taken him completely by surprise...in so many ways.

Long minutes later she dragged her mouth from his, straining and pulling against her bonds, her breathing ragged. Unable to resist burying his face in the fragrant curve of her neck, he nuzzled her throat. The stubble along his jaw lightly abraded her skin, and he soothed the scrape with a long, slow lap of his tongue.

She inhaled sharply. The handcuffs rattled, and a frustrated sound caught in her throat. "Release me, Dean," she groaned.

Certain they'd carried things too far and much too quickly, he immediately obeyed her request. Disengaging himself from her, he reached up and fumbled with the keys until he found the small silver one that unlocked the cuffs and she was freed.

He rubbed his thumbs across the faint red marks that had chafed her wrists, and swore beneath his breath, feeling instantly contrite for keeping her restrained. "Are you okay?"

"I'm just fine," she said in a low, throaty voice, and pounced at him with startling speed and an astonishing strength that took him completely off guard.

The next thing Dean knew *he* was flat on his back with Jo positioned on top of him, his own hands pinned securely on either side of his head by her vise-like grip and her knees clenching his thighs to keep him immobile beneath her. As if he was going anywhere, even if he could, he thought wryly.

While she was slender in stature, there was no

doubt in his mind that she could take care of herself in a threatening situation. "Is this one of those moves they teach you in the police academy?"

A Cheshire cat smile curved her sweet mouth. "That, and martial arts training comes in handy too." Her rich, disheveled hair spilled around her flushed face, and she gazed down at him, sloe-eyed, relaxed, and mellow, despite the upper hand she'd managed to gain. "Turnabout being fair play and all, I do believe it's *my* turn to have a little fun with the fantasy," she murmured seductively.

Still sitting on his thighs, still banding his wrists with her fingers, she bent over him and let her mouth hover above his for a few heartbeats. Choppy, uneven breaths blended as she drew out the heady anticipation. Eyes met, intense and hypnotic, and he watched as her irises turned a sultry shade of blue.

Finally, she dipped her head and nibbled at his bottom lip, alternately rolling the soft flesh between her teeth and biting gently to stimulate and arouse. Her velvet soft tongue joined the sensual assault, but stopped short of entering his mouth. She dabbled, tasted, and explored without completely fusing their lips, deliberately driving him wild with her sweet but, oh, so erotic ministrations.

Her hands gradually relaxed their hold and released his wrists. As her mouth continued to seduce his, she skimmed her fingertips down his arms, over his straining biceps, then flattened her palms on his naked chest and brushed her thumbs over his rigid nipples. Unable to take any more of her teasing, he cupped the back

"*This* time, anyway," he replied with a presumptuous smile.

He knew he sounded confident, but didn't care. After what had just transpired between them it was pointless to deny their attraction, absurd to believe there wouldn't be another hot, sexy encounter in their near future. Not if he could help it.

She didn't deny it, either.

They'd come to a turning point that had everything to do with the trust they'd given each other moments ago on the bed. Her to him, and him to her. And he planned to take the awareness between them as far as she was willing to let it go. There was no doubt in his mind that he wanted Jo—stripped naked, wet, silky and hot—flowing over him, writhing beneath him, wrapped tight around him. In every erotic way he could take her. With her just as restless and needy as he.

In a very short amount of time she'd become a fever in his blood, one he suspected would take a hell of a lot more than a single sexual coupling to shake. With a week-long break looming in front of him and nowhere else he'd rather be, not only did he have the opportunity to learn more about Jo Sommers, but the vacation afforded him the opportunity to take each sizzling encounter one tryst at a time until they figured out where it would all lead. To a mutually satisfying, temporary affair, he wondered, or something much deeper and more lasting?

By the end of the week, they'd both know the answer to that question.

"So, Ms. Sommers," he drawled, deciding to place the next move into her capable hands. "Where do we go from here?"

She mulled over the deliberate double meaning of his question, then gave a casual shrug of her shoulder. "We head back to San Francisco to clear your name."

He grinned. She may have opted for a sensible, practical response, but the undeniable desire still evident in the depths of her eyes left the possibility of a wicked seduction wide open.

AFTER PACKING UP their belongings into the Suburban, checking out of the motel, and grabbing two large coffees and breakfast sandwiches at the same fast-food restaurant they'd driven through the night before, they were back on Interstate 5 heading through Oregon to California. According to Jo, she calculated that they'd arrive in the late afternoon. If she kept up her current seventy-mile-per-hour pace, Dean had no doubt she'd meet her estimated time of arrival, despite the gray, leaden skies that had been threatening rain for the past two hours.

Nearly three hundred miles out of Kelso, Washington, and halfway to their destination, Dean came to the conclusion that while Jo had no qualms about indulging in light, easy conversation to get better acquainted with him, she was incredibly adept at avoiding sharing any kind of deep, intimate information about herself. Especially when it came to imparting the details of her dream last night.

Whatever the source of that nightmare, just mentioning the sleep-induced terror she'd experienced made her grow tense and clam up. When he'd been straightforward enough to push the issue and asked who Brian was, all she'd revealed, albeit reluctantly and with a hint of pain and guilt in her voice, was that he'd been her partner, and had been shot and killed while they'd attempted to take a suspected child kidnapper into custody.

That had been the end of *that* particular story, even though Dean suspected a whole lot more had transpired during the incident. But like a well-trained cop turned P.I., she'd easily and skillfully turned the conversation and questions back to him. She'd extracted more information about his boring, mundane life in Seattle than any normal person would be interested in hearing, but the light verbal exchange took her mind off her nightmare and made her relax and smile again, so he hadn't minded being the source of her distraction.

But long hours and even longer miles still stretched ahead of them, and he was all talked out about himself and still too curious about this slender but tough-as-nails woman who made a living capturing criminals bold enough to jump bail.

He glanced her way, silently taking in the graceful lines of her profile set against the darkness of the oncoming storm gathering outside the windows, at the long, dark lashes that framed expressive eyes, and her small, perfectly sculpted nose that blended into high, delicate cheekbones. And then there were her shapely lips, so soft and warm and seductive, which could be so hot and erotic and addictive. The shape of her face ended with a small chin that had revealed shades of stubbornness, as well as the kind of vulnerability he'd witnessed last night when she'd cuddled up to him after her bad dream.

She'd changed into a pair of jeans and a button-down blouse, and had opted to leave her holster off and her weapons stowed beneath her seat for now. She wore minimal makeup, her hair was gathered back into a ponytail, and he decided he preferred the strands loose around her shoulders. All in all, she was truly lovely, a female paradox so opposite to the hard-edged, jaded image of a bounty hunter most people conjured in their minds.

As if sensing his gaze on her, she turned her head and smiled. "Are you doing okay?"

After nearly five hours on the road with only one bathroom stop and one measly breakfast sandwich to hold him over until his next meal, his stomach was beginning to growl for food. "I am starting to get a little hungry for lunch," he admitted.

"You're like a bottomless pit," she teased, reaching for the trip ticket tucked in her visor. She spared a quick look at the map outlining the route home and the stops in between. "Can you hang in there for another hour and a half when we stop to fill up with gas in Medford? I'd really like to make it that far and take care of everything in one stop."

The woman was a relentless driver, pushing for maximum miles in one stretch. Then again, her penchant for speed was to his benefit; the sooner they arrived in San Francisco, the quicker his identity would become his again.

"The longer you make me wait, the more it's gonna cost you," he said, reminding her of his ravenous appetite last night.

Her laughter filled the interior of the vehicle. "I can afford it." She put the map away and hooked her thumb toward the back of the vehicle. "In the meantime, there are some snacks in a plastic bag behind your seat to hold you over, along with those bottled waters we put on ice before leaving the motel."

Reaching behind his seat, he managed to retrieve the bag she'd mentioned and a bottled water, which he tucked into the drink holder in the center console. Then he rummaged through the contents of the sack and inventoried the variety of junk food.

"Chocolate, chocolate, and more chocolate," he said, finding a common theme among the munchies she'd brought along on her trip. "Geez, Jo, your snack habits are atrocious."

She rolled her eyes. "You're beginning to sound like my brother, Cole. I've been listening to him nag at me about my preference of snacks since I was a teenager."

He pulled out three kinds of cookies: chocolate chip, chocolate-striped shortbread, and chocolate-covered graham crackers. "Obviously, he had every right to nag," he said wryly.

She took her gaze off the road for a moment to crinkle her adorable nose at him. "Judging by what you ate last night, you're certainly not a health food nut yourself.''

''No, but my meals consist of more than just chocolate.''

''And chocolate is a daily part of my diet,'' she stated with mock seriousness, ''so hand over the chocolate shortbread and no one will get hurt.''

He chuckled, enjoying the playful banter between them. ''Those are the ones I wanted, so we're gonna have to share.''

Beads of rain splattered the windshield, and she switched on the wipers to clear the front window. ''You're lucky I like you, or else you know there would be no contest over who'd get those cookies.''

Remembering the efficient way she'd wrestled him to the bed earlier that morning, he didn't doubt her claim. ''Now that could be fun, especially in such a small space.'' He looked around the close quarters of the front seat of the truck and waggled his brows at her.

A becoming flush swept over her cheeks. ''Hmm, and very cramped.''

''Cramped isn't necessarily a bad thing. Makes for a tighter fit.'' Tight, hot, and no doubt very, very exciting. Keeping the bag of shortbread cookies, he tossed the rest of the snacks behind the seat. ''Ever done it in a car before?''

She shook her head incredulously. ''I thought we were talking about *cookies*.''

''We were, along with you wrestling me for them, which made me think of all the interesting kinds of positions two people could get into in a car, which made me think of having sex in a car." Specifically, with her.

She arched a brow his way. "Have *you?*"

"I asked you first," he drawled, not allowing her to turn the question back to him until he had her answer first.

Her fingers curled around the steering wheel, and she stared straight ahead as the wipers swished back and forth. "No, I've never gone all the way in a car before. Just necking and petting." Finally, she slanted a curious look his way. "Have you?"

"I've made it as far as third base in the back seat of a car with my senior prom date, but never all the way," he admitted with a grin. "But there's a first time for everything, even making love in a car, don't you think?"

She inhaled deeply. Her chest rose and her taut nipples grazed the material of her blouse, confirming that the thought thrilled her as much as it did him. "I'm thinking we shouldn't venture down that particular path," she said in a practical tone.

Lifting his hand, he stroked his fingers down the side of her neck, loving the feel of her soft skin and the way his touch made her shiver. "Don't discount anything between us, Jo," he murmured huskily, meaningfully.

"I'm not discounting anything at all." Her reply was candid and portentous, matching the sexy, brazen smile quirking the corner of her mouth. "I just meant that this probably isn't the best conversation to have right now, considering the long drive ahead of us."

He winked at her. "We could consider it verbal foreplay."

She shifted restlessly in her seat, seemingly already hot and bothered by their discussion. "How about we save that arousing subject matter for another time, when I don't have to concentrate on driving in the rain?" she suggested prudently. "Now hand over a cookie and a change of subject, please."

Satisfied that she was fully, sensually aware of him, despite her request to temporarily end their sexy debate, he granted her wish. "Change of subject coming up, along with junk food." He ripped open the bag of shortbread treats, and the scent of rich milk chocolate permeated the air. "How long have you been a bounty hunter?" he asked conversationally.

"The politically correct term is bail recovery agent," she said, the amusement in her voice telling him that his choice of topic was one she was comfortable talking about. "I've been around the business since I was seventeen, but I've only been an actual certified agent for the past two years. I went for training and my license after I quit the police force and went to work for my brother, Cole, at his investigative firm."

Pulling a cookie from the bag, he bit it in half and lifted the other section to Jo's mouth. When she gave him a perplexed look, he smiled and said, "You drive, and I'll keep the supply of chocolate coming."

She opened her mouth and accepted his offering

and he deliberately let his fingers linger on her bottom lip. "Thank you," she murmured, and chewed the confection.

"You're welcome." He licked the taste of chocolate and the sweetness of Jo from his thumb. "I have to say, seventeen seems kind of young to be exposed to such a rough business, considering you're dealing with dangerous criminals." He couldn't imagine allowing a daughter or sister of his to take an active interest in the search and seizure of delinquents. "Or is that what your dad does for a living?"

She accepted another half-eaten cookie, and shook her head. "No, my father is dead. He was a police officer, too, and was shot and killed in the line of duty when I was sixteen. For the most part Cole raised me after that, though my other brother, Noah, helped out, too, until he joined the Marines six months after my dad passed away."

He contemplated her answer, and realized one crucial element was missing. "Where was your mother during all this?"

Her lips flattened into a grim line. "That's a story all in itself."

He heard the tinge of bitterness in her voice, and discovered the need to understand its source. "I'm all ears."

She tipped her head in his direction, her gaze flickering with doubt. "You sure you want to hear all the sordid details of my unorthodox family life?"

"I wouldn't ask if I wasn't interested." And he didn't think her life could be any more dysfunctional than his own had been. "Besides, you're the one who didn't want to talk about sex," he reminded her, flashing an irresistible grin. "And we've got a good hour and a half to fill."

"All right," she conceded, "and when I see you nodding off I'll know you've heard enough of my boring tale."

"I can't imagine anything about you boring me, sweetheart, but give it your best shot." He filled her mouth with the other half of the cookie he'd nibbled on.

She chewed and swallowed, seemingly gathering her thoughts. "My mother and father divorced when I was five, which wasn't so surprising considering they were always arguing about something. From what Cole has told me, my mom was having an affair with a guy she worked with, and when Peter Shaw was offered an intercompany transfer to Prescott, Arizona, Melinda decided to end her current marriage to my dad to go with him."

"And you and your brothers stayed with your father?" he guessed.

"No. It wasn't enough that my mother was leaving my father for another man, she wanted to make him suffer even more than that and used me as a way to hurt my father because she knew I was daddy's little girl. I adored my father. He was always larger than life to me." She brushed errant cookie crumbs from her jean-clad thigh. "Anyway, my mother fought and won full custody of me, left my older brothers with my dad, and off we went to Arizona, where I was ignored for the most part because my mother was so caught up in her new marriage.''

Compassion welled up in him. ''That must have been pretty difficult for all of you, being separated like that.''

She nodded. ''Yeah, it was. I can remember feeling so lost and confused and homesick for my dad and brothers, but I was only allowed to see them during summer vacation. That pattern went on for three years, until my mother was killed in a car accident.''

''I take it your dad was finally granted custody?''

''Not at first, and not easily.'' Lightning flashed outside the vehicle, followed by an ominous rumble of thunder as the storm unleashed its fury and the black clouds overhead finally let loose a downpour of rain.

''What happened?'' he asked.

''Peter held on to me for six months, fighting for custody of me in some warped way to hang on to my mother's memory,'' she went on, slowing her speed and switching the wipers to high to keep up with the steady downpour. ''But he ultimately lost any rights, thank goodness. I was eight at the time, and when I returned to Oakland to live permanently with my dad, both of my brothers became very protective of me. Especially Cole, who was the one who took on a good part of the responsibility of raising me since our father worked varying shifts for the police department.''

He pilfered another cookie to share. ''I'm not surprised that he was protective of you, considering you were the baby of the family, the only girl, and you all had been separated for three years."

She narrowed her gaze at him, that he dared to side with her overbearing sibling. "I couldn't even go to the bathroom without letting Cole know where I was off to," she said, an exaggeration, Dean was certain. "Trust me, the coddling and the constant sentinel was overkill."

Only to a very independent, stubborn young girl who'd grown into an equally obstinate woman, he thought with a mild degree of amusement he knew better than to express.

Twisting the top off the water bottle, he took a long drink. Once his thirst was quenched he said, "Back to my original question. How did you learn the tricks of the bounty hunter trade, especially at the tender young age of seventeen?"

"Bail recovery," she reminded him with a half grin. Accepting the plastic bottle he held out to her, she took a generous swallow. "Cole was twenty-one when my father died, and at the time he was going to college during the day to get his degree in criminal justice and working part-time at night as a bouncer at a local dance club. Since I was a minor, Cole had to apply for guardianship, which he was granted, but he also realized he now had to support me and my brother."

"Did he quit college?"

"Cole?" Her voice held a cynical note, underscored with reluctant pride. "No, he managed to juggle school while raising me and my brother, and holding down a full-time job. He's the most single-minded, ambitious person I know—to the point that he has tunnel vision, never deviating from his goals, or work, or what he believes is expected of him.''

Jo could have been talking about *him*. "Hey, I know someone like that.''

"At least you're beginning to realize that there's more to life than the next project, case, or contract.'' Warmth and humidity from the outside storm found its way into the truck, and Jo turned the air-conditioning on low to ward off the tropical heat. "I don't hold out the same hope for Cole. He's been programmed to be the responsible one for so long, he doesn't know how to stop and smell the flowers or, in his case, see that his own secretary is hot for him.''

Dean's brows rose in surprise. "Really?''

"Yeah, really.'' She shook her head in disgust at her brother's inability to take note of a woman's obvious interest in him. "Then again, the mere fact that Melodie Turner is the daughter of the man who was once my father's sergeant and best friend, and still a mentor for Cole, would make Mel off-limits to my dense brother anyway.''

A chuckle escaped from Dean. He couldn't wait to meet her brother and form his own opinion of the man, which he suspected would differ drastically from Jo's.

"Back to my story,'' she said, putting the conversation on its original track. "After my father died, Cole went to work for a private investigator who was a good friend of my dad's, mostly doing surveillance and security work and learning the ins and outs of the business while finishing up his degree. In order to earn extra money, he started picking up recovery cases from a local bondsman. And because Noah was off in the Marines, there were times when Cole had to take me along on a job during the summer months when I wasn't in school because there wasn't anyone to watch me, and he didn't want to leave me alone.'' She cast him a quick glance and seemingly read the thoughts filtering through his mind. ''Yeah, I know it was kinda unethical taking a minor on those runs, but as a teenager who led a sheltered life thanks to my brother's overprotectiveness, I thought it was cool.''

He heard the undeniable excitement in her voice and couldn't help the smile that formed. ''And that's how you learned the business?''

She nodded, staring ahead as her headlights slashed through the heavy deluge of rain. ''That was the start of it, and spending that time with Cole made me realize how much I enjoy the chase and capture, but of course I was too young at the time to actually help him in any way, not that he'd have let me get involved, even if I'd wanted to.'' She took another drink of water, licked the droplets of water from her lips with her tongue, and continued. ''Over the years, Cole continued picking up bail recovery jobs, and even saved up enough money to put me through college and open his own investigative company. And I have to say, after raising me for so many years, he wasn't too thrilled when I decided I wanted to go into law enforcement, like our father.''

He munched into another cookie, wondering if she'd been out to prove something when she'd made that decision, and slipped the other half of the chocolate-covered shortbread into her mouth. ''You were his baby sister and I'm sure he worried about you getting hurt.''

''Being his baby sister is just one of the many strikes against me,'' she said around a mouthful of cookie, followed by a frustrated sigh. ''Being female doesn't help, as well as a featherweight, as my other brother, Noah, so fondly loves to call me.''

He tipped his head, amused and curious at the same time. '''Featherweight'?''

''Yeah, as in small, delicate, and petite,'' she told him.

He took in her slender but toned stature, liking the package he saw. ''From my viewpoint, it's not a bad combination.''

She gave a very unladylike snort of disagreement. ''My size and gender have always put me at a disadvantage with my brothers, especially when I made the decision to become a police officer. A lot of my colleagues, and even the men I dated, didn't believe I was capable of handling the risk and rigors of the job.'' Her voice trailed off and she glanced out the driver's side window, away from him and toward the Oregon mountains surrounding them. ''And I suppose I proved them right,'' she added in an aching whisper that was so soft he wasn't sure the painful comment had been meant for his ears to hear.

He remained quiet, waiting for her to offer more, but her continued silence indicated that she wasn't willing to share an explanation. And when she looked back at him and he was privy to the grief and sadness in her eyes, he realized he wasn't willing to push the issue.

A slow smile chased away some of the anguish he'd witnessed. "More than you wanted to know about me, I'm sure," she murmured.

"Not at all." If anything, she'd only whet his interest. He saw her as a woman struggling for her own individual identity, acceptance of herself, and respect for her abilities. After learning about her turbulent childhood and her free-spirited nature being tamped, he understood why.

Yet he suspected she was hiding other secrets, too, and he wanted to uncover them all, layer by intriguing layer.

"I'd like to know a whole lot more," he said, his voice low and deeply genuine. "Anything and everything I can learn about you, Jo Sommers."

She laughed, her fingers idly tracing the grooves in the steering wheel. "After the conversation we just had, I don't think there's much left to learn."

"Sure there is," he drawled, undaunted by her attempt to curb his deliberate interest. "Like, is your real name Jo, or is it short for something else?"

Surprise lit her eyes at his uncomplicated, casual question. Obviously, she'd been expecting something

PLAY LUCKY 7 and get FREE Gifts!

Lucky 7

HOW TO PLAY:

1. With a coin, carefully scratch off the gold area at the right. Then check the claim chart to see what we have for you — **2 FREE BOOKS** and a **FREE GIFT** — **ALL YOURS FREE!**

2. Send back the card and you'll receive two brand-new Harlequin Blaze® novels. These books have a cover price of $4.50 each in the U.S. and $5.25 each in Canada, but they are yours to keep absolutely free.

3. There's no catch. You're under no obligation to buy anything. We charge nothing — **ZERO** — for your first shipment. And you don't have to make any minimum number of purchases — not even one!

4. The fact is, thousands of readers enjoy receiving books by mail from the Harlequin Reader Service®. They enjoy the convenience of home delivery...they like getting the best new novels at discount prices, BEFORE they're available in stores...and they love their *Heart to Heart* subscriber newsletter featuring author news, horoscopes, recipes, book reviews and much more!

5. We hope that after receiving your free books you'll want to remain a subscriber. But the choice is yours — to continue or cancel, any time at all! So why not take us up on our invitation, with no risk of any kind. You'll be glad you did!

We can't tell you what it is...but we're sure you'll like it! A surprise **FREE GIFT** just for playing LUCKY 7!

visit us online at
www.eHarlequin.com

NO COST! NO OBLIGATION TO BUY!

NO PURCHASE NECESSARY!

Scratch off the gold area with a coin. Then check below to see the gifts you get!

Lucky 7

YES! I have scratched off the gold area. Please send me the 2 Free books and gift for which I qualify. I understand I am under no obligation to purchase any books as explained on the back and on the opposite page.

350 HDL DNKJ   150 HDL DNJ7

| FIRST NAME | LAST NAME |

ADDRESS

| APT.# | CITY |

| STATE/PROV. | ZIP/POSTAL CODE |

(H-B-04/02)

Worth **2 FREE BOOKS** plus a **FREE GIFT!**

Worth **2 FREE BOOKS!**

Worth **1 FREE BOOK!**

Try Again!

Offer limited to one per household and not valid to current Harlequin Blaze® subscribers. All orders subject to approval.

The Harlequin Reader Service® — Here's how it works:

Accepting your 2 free books and gift places you under no obligation to buy anything. You may keep the books and gift and return the shipping statement marked "cancel." If you do not cancel, about a month later we'll send you 4 additional books and bill you just $3.80 each in the U.S., or $4.21 each in Canada, plus 25¢ shipping & handling per book and applicable taxes if any.* That's the complete price and — compared to cover prices of $4.50 each in the U.S. and $5.25 each in Canada — it's quite a bargain! You may cancel at any time, but if you choose to continue, every month we'll send you 4 more books, which you may either purchase at the discount price or return to us and cancel your subscription.

*Terms and prices subject to change without notice. Sales tax applicable in N.Y. Canadian residents will be charged applicable provincial taxes and GST.

If offer card is missing write to: Harlequin Reader Service., 3010 Walden Ave., P.O. Box 1867, Buffalo NY 14240-1867

BUSINESS REPLY MAIL
FIRST-CLASS MAIL   PERMIT NO. 717-003   BUFFALO, NY

POSTAGE WILL BE PAID BY ADDRESSEE

HARLEQUIN READER SERVICE
3010 WALDEN AVE
PO BOX 1867
BUFFALO NY 14240-9952

NO POSTAGE
NECESSARY
IF MAILED
IN THE
UNITED STATES

more personal. "My full name is Joelle, and my brothers shortened it to Jo when I was a baby." She shrugged. "The nickname kinda carried on through the years."

"Joelle," he repeated, testing her given name on his tongue and enjoying how soft and feminine it sounded. "I like it. It's beautiful and unique, just like you, while Jo suits your determined, obstinate, and confident side."

She grinned wryly. "Thank you, I think."

"It was meant as a compliment, and you're welcome," he replied, watching as she glanced down at the gauges on the control panel in front of her, which she seemed to be checking more and more often the past hour. When a slight, concerned frown marred her brows, he asked, "Is everything okay?"

"I'm not sure." Her gaze ventured from the panel, to the rain-slicked road ahead, then back again. "For some reason, the temperature gauge is starting to run hotter than normal."

They continued on despite her worry, but half an hour later it was obvious that something was very wrong. With the temperature needle climbing steadily into the red danger zone, and the first signs of steam rising from the front of the Suburban, there was no doubt in either of their minds that there was a problem with the engine.

They passed a sign indicating an upcoming off-ramp seemingly out in the middle of nowhere, and since Medford was still a good fifteen miles away, Jo was forced to make a split-second decision. "I'm going to have to pull off this exit and get us to a gas station.''

There was no sign of life in either direction, so she took a chance and made a right turn. The unevenly paved road wound its way through dense forests of trees, broken by occasional hills and green land and pastures…and nothing else. Two miles off the interstate, the vehicle gave a huge jarring shudder, and the engine shut down, forcing Jo to coast the mechanical beast to the gravel shoulder of the road where they came to their final resting place.

She glared up at the furious, stormy sky and blew an upward stream of breath that made the loose tendrils of hair around her face flutter against her forehead. ''Dammit,'' she muttered, clearly annoyed at their less-than-desirable predicament. ''What the hell could be wrong? Cole just had the truck serviced last month.''

''It's probably something no one could have caught ahead of time,'' he said, opting for a practical excuse. ''I'll go check under the hood and see what, if anything, I can find wrong.''

He reached for the door handle, ready to brave the driving rain for her, but she grabbed the sleeve of his shirt to hold him back. ''I'll do it.''

The mutinous tilt to her chin didn't bode well for an argument on his end, yet he wasn't about to sit in the car while she checked the engine, no matter how good her mechanical skills might be. ''A second pair of eyes can't hurt, Jo.''

She hesitated, then finally realizing that he wasn't

going to back down, she relented. "Fine." Unlatching her lap belt, she twisted around and flattened the back seat so she could crawl to the back cargo area. Opening a side compartment, she retrieved a rag, flashlight and an umbrella, then returned to the cab. "If you insist on coming out in the deluge, then you can hold the umbrella while I'm looking under the hood so we don't get drenched."

He rolled his eyes at the token assignment she'd given him, which left her in charge, of course. Fine, he'd cede control, trust in her abilities, and let her run this particular show her way, and not be the kind of overbearing macho male she abhorred.

It took Jo less than two minutes to discover the blown radiator hose that had led to their breakdown, while Dean did his best to shelter them from the elements of the storm. Thunder rumbled overhead, and lightning struck too close for comfort, startling them both. Since there wasn't anything they could do about the fractured hose until they were towed to a service station, they shut the hood and slipped back inside the safety of the vehicle.

Their clothes were damp, and without the air-conditioning, warmth and humidity clung in the air and to their skin. Jo retrieved her cell phone to call road service, and swore vividly when she couldn't get a signal and the digital display lit up with an "out of range" message.

"Great," she muttered in defeat, and tucked the offending unit back into the console. "We're stranded in a storm that's going to last who knows how long, with no way to call for help, and on a road that is all but deserted.'' She exhaled a taut breath and glanced his way. ''Now what do we do?''

Unfortunately, he didn't have any magical answers for her, but he was a resourceful kind of guy, and that meant grasping the opportunity to relax and enjoy the next couple of hours with each other until the weather cleared and they were able to walk ahead and find help.

Seduction and surrender beckoned, and remembering their earlier conversation about making out in a car, he reached out and trailed his fingers along her shoulder and down her bare arm. ''Now that you no longer have to concentrate on driving, I'm thinking we could test out the back seat area and have a little fun until the storm passes. Just a little necking and petting and whatever else you'd like to do.'' He grinned slowly, sinfully, meaningfully, but left the final decision up to her. ''What do you say, Jo?''

He watched her swallow as she considered his idea and all the sensual possibilities awaiting them if she agreed to his tantalizing suggestion. He longed to indulge in the kind of pleasing, arousing recreation they'd both enjoyed back at the motel before they'd been stopped by her alarm clock and the need to get back on the road.

He saw the tension in her body from being stranded gradually fade away, replaced by desire and an undeniable excitement flaring to life in the depths of her eyes. ''I'm game if you are,'' she whispered, and made good on her own daring response by being the first one to climb into the back of the Suburban.

8

JO SETTLED onto her knees on the soft, flannel blanket she'd spread out in the cargo area, and waited for Dean to join her. Her gaze scanned the space, taking in her traveling gear, the cooler, and their baggage, which she'd pushed up against the sides of the truck to make more room for them in the middle. There was a good six feet of cleared space, more than enough for her to stretch out on, but it would no doubt come up a few inches short for Dean.

She caught sight of her unusable cell phone, a direct, unwanted reminder of everything that awaited her back home. Reality, and a strict, by-the-book brother who'd never trust the choice she was about to make, no matter that Dean was an innocent man.

Undoubtedly, Cole would be concerned if he tried to call and couldn't reach her, believing she was out of reach and possibly in trouble with a convicted felon. He'd worry as any sibling would, but ultimately he'd have to believe in her and her instincts and abilities, which was a difficult feat for Cole when it came to her, she knew.

But right now, at this very moment, she wanted to forget everything but this man she was highly attracted to. She didn't want to think about Cole or the lecture she was in store for, or how everyone questioned her judgment for the past two years, herself included. She wasn't questioning her choice with Dean anymore. She was taking back control of a part of her life she'd lost after Brian's death. Now, she wanted, *needed,* to feel alive and desirable, and Dean Colter made that possible.

Her entire body pulsed in awareness as Dean wedged his way through the opening and the earthy scent of him filled her senses. Figuring there was no point in being shy, modest, or coy, she shook off every inhibition she'd ever possessed. Sexually and physically, he thrilled and aroused her. Emotionally and personally, he seemed to understand her more than any man ever had, and that was an equal turn-on for her.

After taking off his wet shoes and socks, as she'd already done, he knelt in front of her and braced his hands on his spread thighs, which brought her attention to the blatant erection already straining the fly of his jeans. She swallowed to ease the dryness in her throat. Every bit of him was big, solid, and male, and she instinctively knew that whatever happened between them this afternoon would be like nothing she'd ever experienced before.

Dean was a man who could give her everything she craved on a purely physical level, satisfy all the pleasures she'd denied herself for years, but would make no demands on her when their time together came to an end in a few days. They lived in separate states, led very different lives. Neither one of them was looking for a commitment or strings and she felt selfish enough to take this encounter to the extreme because no man had ever made her feel or want so much. After spending the past two years trying to prove her self-worth and focusing on her abduction cases, she was going to put her needs first and please herself for a change.

And being with Dean pleased her greatly.

Reaching out, she spread her hand on his chest, absorbing his rapid heartbeat and the scorching heat of him through the rain-dampened cotton of his T-shirt. She trailed a finger over a rigid nipple and his eyes darkened with fiery hunger.

Her heart skipped an exciting beat. The fury of the storm continued to pelt the vehicle with loud droplets, creating a lush, provocative staccato that heightened the sensuality between them. The shelter of the tall trees around the car, coupled with the gray skies above and the steady moisture drizzling down all the windows, added to the eroticism of their encounter. It also cocooned them from the outside forces and any prying eyes that might happen upon them.

She cast him a slow smile. "It's definitely cramped back here," she said, referring to their earlier conversation and all the interesting positions two people could manage in tight spaces.

He blinked lazily, which did nothing to bank the gold hue of desire flaring in the depths of his eyes. "We'll be creative and make it work any way we have to."

Gazes locked, her fingers skimmed their way down to his lean, flat abdomen, which flexed at her touch. "And it's warm and humid inside the truck, too." Her voice was low and breathy.

"Makes for better friction when it comes to skin-on-skin contact." His palms remained planted on his thighs, but his words and the deep timbre of his voice were as erotic as a caress. "Take the elastic band from your ponytail for me, Jo. I want your hair down."

Unable to refuse him anything, she did as he requested and rolled the band off and let her hair fall free about her shoulders. Leaning forward, he plowed all ten fingers through the damp strands and pulled her face toward his.

Her eyelids fluttered closed and her lips parted seconds before his mouth claimed hers in a hot, open-mouthed kiss. A soft moan escaped her as she welcomed the silky invasion of his tongue and appreciated the enticing taste of scrumptious shortbread cookies and masculine possession. He took her deeper and deeper into the kiss—ravishing her mouth with his lips and teeth, mating their tongues, stealing her very breath—until all coherent thought fled her mind.

"Your shirt," she panted against his soft, damp lips as she tugged the material from the waistband of his jeans. "I want it off."

In one fluid motion he gripped the hem, pulled it over his head, and tossed the shirt aside. "Better?"

"Oh, much." She placed her hands on his well-defined chest, not at all surprised when her own breasts swelled at the contact. She stroked his smooth skin and firm muscle, and leaned close to scatter warm, moist kisses along his jaw, run the tip of her tongue down his neck, and suck the pulsing skin at the base of his throat.

His entire body shuddered, and he gathered her hair in his fists as her lips coasted over his chest and she tasted the salt on his skin and inhaled the intoxicating scent of aroused male. She deliberately grazed her teeth across his erect nipples and heard him draw in a swift breath, felt the tiny nub of flesh harden even more against her curled tongue.

Before she could continue her journey downward, he urged her with his hands to sit back up. Breathing hard, they stared at each other as a clap of thunder shook the vehicle with the sheer force of the loud boom that reverberated across the Oregon sky. A torrent of rain followed, and he fused their mouths yet again as he shifted his body and eased her down onto the blanket. He stretched out beside her and hooked his knee across her legs to accommodate the length of his frame in the small space.

He slowed their kisses, and in his own good time unfastened the first button on her blouse, then another, and yet another, making her restless with his slow, drawn-out movements—making her dizzy with the anticipation of experiencing his sweeping caress on her exposed flesh. Once done, he pulled the ends of her opened blouse from her jeans, and she shivered when his mouth glided across the full swells of her bra-encased breasts. He continued to nibble his way to the straining peak, and once he reached his destination he tongued the distended nipple pressing against textured lace.

A sense of urgency gripped her, and she nearly fainted with relief when he unclasped the front of her bra and *finally* released her breasts. Letting the cups fall to her sides, he strummed his long fingers over the aching crests, which were excruciatingly stiff from his teasing ministrations, and damp from his wet mouth and the humidity in the truck from the rain outside and the combined body heat inside. Even the windows were fogged from their heavy breathing.

Their eyes met and locked, his dark, smoky gaze heavy-lidded with desire and glittering with something far more primal. He swirled his thumb around a sensitive, still-slick aureole, using the feverish warmth and dampness from her skin to increase the friction against her nipple and heighten the pure, sensual pleasure of his touch.

He grinned knowingly, and a devilish light entered his gaze. "Kinda hot and steamy in here, don't you think?"

"As you can feel for yourself, I'm burning up." She was on fire, and she had a feeling it was going to get a whole lot hotter before they were through.

"Yeah, you are," he agreed huskily as his gaze took in the flush on her skin. "Let's see what we can do about lowering your temperature a little bit."

Pulling the small cooler closer, he flipped it open and rummaged through the chilled drinks. Instead of retrieving a canned soda as she'd expected, he instead slipped a large ice cube into his mouth, then closed his chilled, wet hand over her swollen breast. She sucked in a startled breath as new and unfamiliar sensations rippled through her, at once shocking and thrilling. Before she could push his freezing touch away, he dipped his head and lapped his cold, velvet-soft tongue up the side of her neck, then captured her mouth with his frosty lips.

He swallowed her sultry moan, unfurled his tongue, and let the melting ice cube slide into her mouth. Then he initiated a sensual game of hide and seek with the frozen chip, chasing the piece of ice with their tongues until both their mouths had shared all of its refreshing coolness, then warmed up together again.

The kiss went on, and her tenuous restraint spiraled and splintered, unleashing assertive, wanton urges. Needing to touch him, she let her hands drift everywhere, from his shoulders, to his arms, to his chest, belly and hips, where she encountered the frustrating barrier of his jeans.

He broke their kiss with a harsh groan and inhaled deeply to regain his breath. "Behave yourself," he said, staring down at her with a mock scowl.

She rolled her eyes, completely unfazed by his attempt to intimidate her. "Why do *you* get to have all the fun?"

He tipped his head and quirked a brow. "You mean to tell me you're not having fun?"

A slow smile curved her lips. "I just don't think

the scales are evenly tipped, what with you having the upper hand in all this.'' And she intended to tip them more in her favor.

As she talked, she skimmed her flattened palm along his thigh and came to a stop against the enormous erection nearly bursting the front placket of his jeans. He pulsed with vibrant life against her curved fingers, and a tiny thrill coursed through her that she held such power in her hands, and that she wasn't the only one aroused so intensely. Smiling wickedly, she stroked him in slow, measured strokes. He grew thicker, longer, and hard as granite, and all she could think about was taking all that aggressive male heat into her bare palm, tasting him with her tongue, and being filled like she'd never been filled before.

Intoxicated by the decadent thought, she acted on pure impulse. But the moment her fingers fumbled with his belt buckle to follow through on her personal fantasy, he grasped her wrists and diverted her plans. He kissed her long and hard and deep while pushing her blouse and bra up and over her head. She lifted her arms to help him remove the garments, only to find her hands tangled in the clothing and her arms stretched and anchored firmly above her head by his hold on the twisted material.

She gave an experimental tug, but her hands remained secured and immobile. ''I'm beginning to think you favor a certain erotic fixation.''

''You mean making you a slave to my whims?'' he guessed, staring at her lush breasts and jutting nipples.

Would he ever take her into his mouth, or would he make her beg for that intimate caress? She was close to doing just that. "Otherwise known as bondage."

He feathered his fingers along her side and down to the indentation of her waist, making her shiver from head to toe. "Do you like being tied up like this?"

Her body's eager response wouldn't let her lie. "Yes, but I'd like to touch you more."

He shook his head, found her hand in the folds of her blouse, and laced their fingers tightly together. "If you touch me again like you just did, I'm certain that would be the end of my control."

At least one of them would finally have the luxury of releasing some of the agonizing sexual tension building between them. "And that's a bad thing?"

His thumb swept over the rapid pulsepoint in her wrist, which matched the steady, insistent throb between her thighs. "Yeah, it would be, especially when I want to make sure you're good and well pleased before I let myself go."

She batted her lashes playfully at him, teasing and taunting his restraint. "My, aren't you the gentleman."

"If that's what you'd like to think." He grinned wolfishly, his eyes blazing with a dark, dangerous kind of edge that made her blood quicken in her veins. "Truth be told, it's pure selfishness on my part, because I want to watch you enjoy yourself. And knowing that you're all tied up and a captive to my will turns me on even more. Doesn't all this excite you, even a little bit?''

"What do you think?'' she returned impudently.

"I have my suspicions, but I think I need to be absolutely sure.'' Still holding on to her wrists with one hand, he reached into the cooler again, digging deep into the ice and lingering for long seconds before bringing a large piece of ice to his mouth. This time he crunched the cube into tiny slivers, then dipped his head and took her nipple into his chilled mouth. With his fingers, he pushed her breast up to his lips, taking as much of her as he could at one time, consuming and devouring her with hard, suctioning swirls of his icy tongue across her nipple.

Wild sensation careened through her and spiraled right to the very core of her femininity. She curled her fingers around his and opened her mouth to scream at the staggering contrast of his freezing mouth ravishing her searing flesh, but only a soft mewling sound managed to emerge. He insisted on giving both breasts equal treatment, until she was excruciatingly aroused and a carnal stroke away from climaxing.

She heard him dig into the ice again and moaned, now knowing what to expect. Yet she still inhaled sharply when his dripping wet, frosty-cold fingers touched down on her stomach and traced a languid path over her navel to the waistband of her jeans.

He lifted his head, met her heavy-lidded gaze, and toyed with the top button on her pants. ''Do you want more?'' he murmured, his question packed with a sexual connotation she couldn't misinterpret.

He was leaving the ultimate decision up to her, and just as he claimed to be selfish, she was feeling just as greedy. "Yes...*please*," she whispered in an achy, needy tone.

Without letting go of her restrained hands, and with an efficiency and agility that amazed her, he managed to unzip her jeans, tug them over her hips with a little wriggle of help from her, and shove the denim down to her knees. Surprisingly, he left her pale pink panties on, which were drenched with desire for him, because of him. She tried to shift her lower body to kick the restricting pants off, but he diverted her attempts by wedging his thigh between her knees just below where the heavy material ended, making it so she could only open her legs about an inch.

His hand dipped back into the cooler, and her chest rose and fell as anticipation unfurled within her. Her hands remained bound, her legs equally confined, yet she still trusted him, knew whatever he had planned would be for her benefit and gratification.

Ice cube in hand, he drew a slow, lazy circle around her belly button, then slid the frozen icicle down to her bikini panties and traced the line of her waistband, then back up again. Leaning down, he blew a gust of hot breath over the cool wetness on her skin, and she shuddered uncontrollably.

He placed the cube on her navel, then reached into the insulated chest again. "Be still," he murmured when she squirmed to dislodge the ice.

Her eyes widened. Oh, God, he couldn't be serious, but one look at his determined expression told her he'd meant what he'd said. As the seconds passed and the ice began to melt and drip down the sides of her stomach, she could feel the wintery chill spread all the way up to the puckered tips of her breasts and radiate lower, too. The prickling sensation was highly erotic, and also drove her mad because he'd ordered her not to move.

Her eyes rolled back and she moaned fitfully, but didn't dare writhe as she longed to do. "Dean...it's too cold."

"The ice stays, for now." He brushed his warm lips along her jaw in compensation and whispered huskily in her ear, "Here, I'll give you something else to think about instead."

Easing his hand between her legs, he pressed two icy fingers against the damp, silky panel of her panties. "You're *very* hot here," he said, his sizzling, uneven breaths scorching her flesh. "Let's see what we can do about cooling you off."

She knew what was coming even before he found his way beneath the elastic band, but being prepared didn't make his glacial caress any less shocking or intense. She sucked air into her lungs as his cold, cold fingers delved through slick folds, then filled her completely with one sleek, gliding stroke inside her.

This time, it was Dean who groaned low and harsh as her inner body gripped him tight, then melted and liquified around the invasion of his chilled fingers thrusting into her heated depths. His still-cold thumb

joined in on the seductive foray, gliding firmly, rhythmically across her wet, highly aroused flesh.

A frustrated sob caught in her throat and she
squeezed her eyes shut. She felt as though her body
was being pulled in a dozen different mindless direc-
tions, with so many sensations bombarding her all at
once that she couldn't concentrate on just one feeling.
She wanted her hands free to touch him in return,
wanted to open her legs wider to accommodate a
greater pressure and friction, but her jeans and his
thigh prevented that. Her belly quivered as he built
the tension within her, higher and higher, making the
slowly dissolving ice cube on her stomach tremble
precariously as she fought to keep it in place—just to
prove she could.

"You're holding back," he said, in tune to all the
subtle nuances of her body. "Let it go, Joelle, and
come for me."

He pushed his fingers high, hard and deep. Deliberately, he plied her swollen clitoris, eliciting a hot
tide of passion and clawing need she was helpless to
deny. Her vision blurred. Her muscles ached, drew
tight, then contracted around his fingers as an incredible, powerful orgasm washed over her in crashing
waves of voluptuous pleasure. She pulled against the
material twisted around her restrained wrists to keep
herself from thrashing, and she moaned in low, gasp-
ing pants as the exquisite, soul-stirring bliss consumed her.

Lightning flashed outside, as wild and frenzied as
the electricity that had ignited her nerve endings. As

the echo of thunder ebbed away, and with the soft, soothing patter of rain on the windows, Jo felt herself floating back down to earth, lethargic, sated, and completely, wonderfully spent.

She lifted her lashes and met Dean's hooded gaze. His face was flushed from the warmth and humidity in the car, his jaw clenched, and his eyes were the color of burning, emerald coals. With excruciating slowness, so she felt every inch of his retreat, he removed his fingers from between her thighs. He dropped a quick kiss on her lips and finally untangled her blouse and bra from her arms and set her free.

But she didn't want to be free, not when he'd yet to find his own release after being so generous with hers. And not when she still felt so empty deep inside, despite the fabulous orgasm he'd given her. She lowered her arms and started to turn toward him to take this encounter to its logical, fulfilling conclusion, but stopped when she felt chilled liquid trickle down the side of her stomach.

She laughed lightly, truly amazed at how provocative and stimulating a piece of ice could be, in so many varied ways. "I was a good girl and the ice stayed right where you put it," she told him. "Do you think you could remove it from my belly button now?"

"You were a very good girl," he agreed generously. He swept his gaze downward, and his fingers followed the same path until the tips glided through the moisture on her belly. "The ice is all melted, and I'm suddenly very, very thirsty."

He lowered his head and sipped the water from her navel, then dipped his tongue into the small indentation, probing deep, until there was no more moisture left. Just that quick, just that easily, she began to throb with renewed hunger and desire. But this time, she wanted the satisfaction to be mutual.

His teeth grazed her plump breast, and his fingers skimmed her thigh. Before he could send her on another journey to the heavens without him, she grasped his wrist in one hand to halt his ascent and threaded the fingers of her other hand through his thick, silky hair. She tugged his head up before he could take a straining nipple into his mouth and distract her all over again.

He lifted a dark brow in question, and her heart softened when she realized that he truly expected nothing in return for what he'd given her. Which made her want him even more. "I need you, Dean...inside me."

He shuddered at her candid declaration, yet his gaze clouded over with shades of regret. "God, I want that, too, but I didn't plan my trip thinking I'd need condoms for any reason and I can't and won't risk getting you pregnant."

"I'm on the pill," she said, and seeing the curiosity etching his features, she attempted to explain. "My doctor put me on it a few years ago because stress and anxiety screwed up my hormones and menstrual cycle. It keeps me regular. As for other concerns, it's been a long time since I've been in a relationship."

He smiled and his shoulders relaxed in relief.

"Whatever the reason, sweetheart, I'm extremely grateful." He eased up to his knees beside her, then hesitated. "Just so long as you're sure about this."

"I am." Certainty rang clear in her voice. "And since you're the one who got me into this tangled mess in the first place," she said, indicating the jeans still caught around her knees, "I'm gonna let you take off the rest of my clothes."

He did so, quickly and easily, sweeping denim and silk down her long legs and tossing the garments aside. And moments later, she was lying completely naked on the flannel blanket, with him kneeling between her open, up-drawn legs. His gaze took in every bare, sprawled inch of her, lower and lower until he came to a stop at the most intimate part of her. His chest heaved with labored breaths, and the hungry need she saw reflected on his face made her tummy flutter.

His visual caress was just as arousing as a physical one, making her body tingle with renewed cravings. Yet she felt more than a little vulnerable with him still with his pants on. "Dean, I'm about at the end of my self-control."

A sinful grin claimed his lips. "Good, because that's exactly where I want you." Quicker than she could anticipate, he hooked her legs over his strong arms to keep them apart, lowered his head, and took her intimately with his mouth.

She inhaled a swift, startled breath, and her back arched as sharp, intense pleasure blazed through her. There was nothing slow or leisurely about this seduction. His mouth was hot and ruthless, his tongue insistent and aggressive, allowing no inhibitions, no retreat. He demanded her surrender a second time, and she gave it to him, her climax hitting so hard and fast that she screamed from the sheer force of it buffeting through her body.

He reared back and unbuckled his belt urgently, the skin across his chest damp with perspiration and his muscles flexing with every brisk movement. "I can't wait any longer. I have to have you." He shoved his jeans and briefs down his thighs and off, releasing his erection and letting her see him for the first time fully naked and stunningly aroused.

A tiny thrill shot through her. He was just as magnificently built as she imagined when she'd glimpsed him in the shower the night before. Instead of coming over her in a standard missionary position, he hooked his fingers behind her knees and dragged her closer to him as his own bent legs widened on either side of her hips. He draped her thighs over his, leaned forward, and rubbed the head of his penis over her sensitive folds, sharing slick moisture before entering her an agonizing inch...then stopping.

A strangled sound of distress caught in her throat and her fingers clutched the blankets at her sides. She glanced up at him to beg and plead to end the torment, but the fierce emotions glimmering in his eyes threw her off kilter.

"Dean?" she rasped, wondering if he'd changed his mind. Wondering, too, if they'd gone further than either of them had ever intended. The thought scared her for all it implied—an emotional entanglement she was in no way ready for.

"I want you, Jo Sommers. *All* of you," he said, his voice a low, husky murmur threaded with a possessive note. "Are you ready for that? Are you ready for *me?*"

She shivered, deciphering the true significance behind his questions—and knew he didn't mean sexually ready so much as was she prepared for him to storm her defenses. Right now, at this moment, she was ready for *this,* and accepted the answer to make it happen.

"Yes," she whispered, and slid a hand between her thighs to run the tips of her fingers along the pulsing length nestled halfway within her, making her ache and swell and throb all over again. "I'm ready."

Seemingly satisfied with her response, he drove solidly into her, filling her completely. Their moans of mutual pleasure mingled with another rumble of thunder overhead, with the hard-driving rain that once again pelted the truck. He barely gave her time to adjust to the luxury of that first stroke before he moved over her, using the breadth of his muscular thighs to push her legs farther apart and tilt her hips for a deeper, more intense penetration that made her gasp at the unexpected force.

Eyes glittering with heat, he slipped his hands under her arms, smoothed his palms up her back, and curled his fingers over her shoulders to lock them even tighter. The position made her realize she was well and truly pinned beneath him—face to face, breasts crushed to his chest, and her legs wrapped high around his waist—but in a way that was new and different, so exciting, and incredibly erotic.

"You feel so damn good," he growled, his jaw clenched in obvious restraint, "and I can't hold off much longer."

She glided her hands down his lean, tightly muscled back, all the way to his toned buttocks. "Then don't," she said, urging him to let go.

With a savage groan he slanted his mouth over hers, stealing her breath the same time he rocked forward with unbridled, jolting purpose. His entire body shuddered with the strength and impact of his thrusts, and she urged him further, higher, harder with her hands, mouth and body, unerringly matching his rhythm and stoking the flames of desire burning between them.

Their lovemaking was raw, earthy, and just as untamed as the storm swirling and raging outside of the vehicle. It was just the kind of frenzied joining she wanted. Just what he apparently needed.

Amazingly, she felt that wondrous climb begin again, building to a crescendo that had her writhing beneath him and moaning desperately as her climax slammed into her. He tossed his head back, his hips pumping, grinding, her name a hoarse cry on his lips as he fell over the precipice and came with her.

And this time, as they shared the explosion of heat and lightning and keen sensation, Jo feared that she'd not only given this generous man her body, but a piece of her heart and soul as well.

9

IN ANOTHER FEW MINUTES, he'd wake up Jo. But for now, with her warm, naked body curled up in front of his, the flannel blanket thrown haphazardly over both of their waists and the rain having ebbed to a light drizzle, Dean luxuriated in the satisfaction and contentment settling deep within him. The kind of mind and body relaxation that came in the aftermath of an incredible, mind-blowing release.

Undeniably, the sex had been amazing—hot, steamy and consuming—with him and Jo so in sync that it was as though they'd been lovers for years. Yet beyond the fantastic orgasm that had been the culmination of all their erotic foreplay, something more intimate had flared bright between them, especially toward the end—an emotional connection he'd felt, and one she seemed to struggle against. A caring yet passionate kind of bond he'd been without for all these years and hadn't known had been missing from his life until this woman had seized him—in more ways than one.

Closing his eyes, he buried his face in her hair, loose and flowing over the duffle they shared for a pillow. He inhaled the arousing scent of sated desire, sweet melon, and the rain that had drenched them earlier. The arm he'd draped over her waist tightened possessively, and he realized that this perfect moment of tranquility and companionship with Jo was a stark reminder of all the things he'd sacrificed to keep his father's company solvent—the comfort of having a woman in his life, and a future with a wife and family.

He'd always wanted both, so certain that his own life would be so different from that of his parents. But from the day his fiancée had walked out on him, he'd known that he couldn't risk doing to a wife and children what his own father had done to him and his mother—put them second to his company. Ultimately, he hadn't trusted himself enough to believe he could be any different than his old man when forced to choose between an important business decision or a promise he'd given to a family waiting for him at home.

Avoiding a long-term commitment with a woman had been easy enough to accomplish over the years. Not only did he not have the extra time to pursue a relationship, but no woman, including Lora, had ever piqued his interest the way Jo had. With all her complexities, intriguing inner depths, and candid sensuality, she made him want to take the kind of chances he'd evaded for too long. She made him more determined to put his wants and needs first, above and beyond his dedication to a business he'd taken over out of family obligation, rather than any personal attachment or interest.

But so many confusing, conflicting crossroads still

loomed ahead of him. Difficult choices that affected people depending on him, and more complicated decisions that suddenly included this beautiful, vibrant woman he wasn't willing to walk away from at the end of the week. A woman who stirred deep, dormant emotions and made him want to put her needs first, too, and see where a relationship could lead.

Unfortunately, he suspected that Jo wouldn't be so easily swayed on that front. She was a woman who'd made it abundantly clear that she was self-reliant and fiercely independent. He agreed that she was all that and more—including emotionally vulnerable and sensitive in a way she'd *never* admit—yet he couldn't shake the notion that she was trying to prove something, to herself, her brothers and any man who tried to get too close. Himself included.

She might be uninhibited when they made love, but he had private, personal barriers to scale with her. He'd meant what he'd said when he'd told her that he wanted all of her, then asked if she was ready for that, ready for him. In his opinion, her answer of yes, no matter spoken under sexual duress, gave him permission to insinuate himself in her life, at least for the next six days. And if it meant using sex to scratch the surface of something deeper during the course of their time together, he'd gladly pay the price.

He lifted his arm from her waist and cast a quick glance at his wristwatch. He'd let her rest for an hour now, giving her extra minutes of peaceful sleep after her restless night in the motel, while he'd remained awake, alternating between watching her and trying to dissect the errant thoughts tumbling through his mind. He hated like hell to disturb her tranquil, untroubled slumber, but he had no idea if there was another storm heading in on the heels of the one that had just passed, or how far they had to walk for help.

Reluctantly, he trailed his fingers down her arm to awaken her gently. "Jo," he said softly, and brushed a tender kiss on her bare shoulder. "You need to wake up so we can get dressed and go find help." And nourishment, he thought wryly. He was starved for more than just chocolate.

She stirred lazily, stretching her lush body along his already aroused one and tangling their legs in the process. "Do we *have* to go?" she murmured sleepily.

He grinned. He'd stay here forever with her if he could. "I think the storm has finally passed, so it's a good time to venture out."

She turned her head to look at him over her shoulder, using an irresistible pout to sway him. "Let's stay just a little bit longer," she whispered, her lashes drooping slumberously. Reaching back, she pressed her palm to his cheek and scooted her bottom closer to his groin, so that his full erection slipped into the warm, damp crease between her slender thighs.

A sultry heat welcomed him, and he was weak enough to admit that her already primed body was all the incentive he needed to agree to her cajoling request. He nibbled on her lobe, traced his tongue along the shell of her ear and cupped a breast in his hand.

Her nipple instantly hardened against his palm. "You're absolutely insatiable."

She arched, wriggling her very feminine posterior against his hips and thighs and pushing her breast more fully into his hand as he delicately plucked the stiff peaks with his fingers. "I've got a lot of lost time to make up for," she said, her tone sensually charged and unapologetic. "And judging by your eager response, I do believe you're more than willing to accommodate my desires."

He gave her nipple one last pinch, then ran his hand down the slope of her smooth back. "Oh, yeah, more than willing," he growled against her neck, and felt a shiver of anticipation course through her.

He tossed off the flannel blanket and moved closer against her backside. Using his knee, he nudged her left leg forward and up, spreading her legs and holding her open for his possession. Grasping her hip to hold her in place, and aching to be inside her again, he rubbed his thickened penis against her swollen flesh, then pushed upward, sinking into her and relishing the feel of her heat and softness enveloping him.

Unlike the urgency of their last joining, this time his strokes were unhurried, deep and long. Lazy. Rhythmic. Designed to build the pressure and heighten her awareness of him, of them, together. A low moan of distress escaped her throat when he pulled back and nearly withdrew, then she sighed gratefully at his slow, smooth slide back inside. Her bottom tilted to take more of him, to urge him to take more of her, but he instead dragged his open mouth along her shoulder, intending to draw out the pleasure, no matter how much the sexy, undulating movements of her body insisted otherwise.

When he retreated yet again, she whimpered and grabbed onto the blanket, using the heel of her hands to push herself back into him the only way she could. "Dean...I need..."

He thrust back into her, stealing the rest of her words as he filled her completely in one fluid stroke. Knowing exactly what she craved, but still determined to do this at his pace, he unfurled her clenched fists and flattened her palm on her stomach, then guided her hand downward, until their entwined fingers glided through damp curls, caressed petal-soft folds of flesh, and gathered the moisture from their joined bodies to use as a silky lubricant.

She tensed, her uncertainty in touching herself in front of him evident in the stillness of her hand trapped beneath his and in the slow, trembling breaths easing in and out of her chest.

He kissed her temple, tasted the salt of perspiration on her skin. "Don't go all shy on me now, sweetheart," he drawled, persuading her to trust him with gentle humor instead of forceful demands. "Show me what you like, what feels good..."

With an unraveling sigh, she relaxed and taught him the secrets of her body. Let him learn firsthand what pleased her and demonstrated the seductive rhythm that turned her on the most while he continued the slow gyration of his hips, his lazy in-and-out penetration. Within minutes he recognized the signs of her approaching climax, the provocative catch of her breath and the way her inner muscles tightened around his shaft and coaxed him deeper and deeper still. Her intimate caresses built to a faster, more urgent crescendo, and a long, low moan reached his ears. She pushed her bottom against his hips, opened her legs wider, straining and arching into him as she greedily took her own pleasure.

Watching her embrace the orgasm shuddering through her that was a direct result of her own ministrations was the most erotic sight he'd ever seen and sent him soaring over the edge with her. His heart pounded erratically in his chest, and he plunged hard and fast, experiencing a need so raw and untamed that it shook the very foundation of his soul.

And then he was lost…in sensation, ecstasy and everything that was Jo Sommers.

REALITY INTRUDED much too quickly for Jo's liking—and along with it the reminder that she had a man's innocence to prove, and a brother to convince of her competence. The two points were going to be a hard sell to Cole, she knew, considering the evidence Cole believed was stacked against Dean.

Gut instinct didn't account for much when compared to her past actions and she resented the way those mistakes continually overshadowed Cole's views and opinion of her abilities when it came to her doing a job. But contacting her brother was unavoidable, especially when she'd been out of reach for hours, and just as soon as they reached some kind of civilization, took care of the truck, and found a place to stay for the night, she'd make that dreaded call.

After forty-five minutes of walking in sprinkling, misty rain while sharing an umbrella, the farmhouse that finally came into sight as the two of them crested a hill had Jo releasing a tired and grateful, "Thank God!" The skies above were gray and leaden, the weather humid and unpredictable, and the threat of yet another storm lingered in the air.

"Thank God is right," Dean agreed, holding the umbrella to protect them against the wet elements as they crossed the deserted highway to the other side of the road where the farmhouse sat in the distance. "I was about to suggest we head back in the opposite direction to the freeway and hitch a ride into Medford."

Jo groaned at the thought of hiking all the way back to the interstate, but the notion had crossed her mind as well considering their limited options. "We got lucky, and hopefully whoever lives here will be able to call us a tow truck and get the Suburban to a service station."

"And us to a restaurant," Dean said, flashing an easygoing grin at her. "I need food. *Real* food."

She sidestepped a puddle between them and was amused when he kept the umbrella over her head and let the rain drizzle on him for that three-second split. "That granola bar just didn't do it for you, huh?" After they'd gotten dressed, they'd eaten another quick snack before heading out for help, just to have something in their stomachs.

He rolled his sexy green eyes. "That *chocolate-covered* granola bar barely put a dent in my appetite," he said wryly.

His physical hunger might still be raging, but their sexual appetites had been mutually appeased, she knew, remembering everything that had transpired in the back area of the truck. The man was an incredible lover, so attentive, generous and passionate. As a result of his focused attention on her and her pleasure, she felt impossibly mellow, every one of her five senses relaxed and wholly satisfied.

They made their way down a well-traveled gravel road bordered by two fenced-in pastures with grazing horses, and passed a newly painted red barn, along with a pen of chickens, goats and a separate garden of fruits and vegetables—a far cry from the hustle and bustle of the city that she was used to. A few minutes later they cleared the front porch steps to the house. While Jo put away the umbrella, Dean rapped his knuckles loudly on the screen door that opened into a living room.

An older man wearing a pair of faded jean overalls appeared in their line of vision. Dean unexpectedly slipped his palm into hers and intertwined their fingers together. She had no idea why he insisted on holding her hand, but she couldn't say she disliked the intimate gesture.

The man stopped on the other side of the door, a frown furrowing his bushy gray brows as he looked

from her to Dean. Not that Jo could blame him for
being wary. No doubt he didn't get many unexpected
visitors at his off-the-beaten-path farmhouse.

"Can I help you?" he asked, his voice deep and
gruff, though his brown eyes reflected a genuine kind-
ness beyond all that caution.

"Who's at the door, Frank?" a soft, feminine voice
interrupted. A plump, pretty older woman with gray-
ing brunette hair came up beside her husband, wiping
her hands on the floral apron wrapped around her
waist as she peered curiously at the two of them.

"Don't know, Iris," Frank replied, pushing his fingers through his thinning gray hair. "That's what I
was trying to find out."

"Hello," the older woman said pleasantly, her
smile warm and friendly. "Are you two lost?"

An engaging grin lifted the corners of Dean's lips.
"Actually, my wife and I are traveling from Seattle
to San Francisco to visit family, and our vehicle broke
down a few miles back with a blown radiator hose,"
he explained to the couple before Jo had the chance
to speak at all. "We were stranded during the storm,
and you're the first sign of civilization we've seen on
this road. We were hoping you could help us out."

His *wife?* Visiting *family* in San Francisco? Jo had
to physically restrain herself from gaping at Dean for
his blatant lie.

"Nope, there isn't much on this stretch of road,"
Frank agreed, scratching his temple. "In fact, the
nearest service station is in Medford, about fifteen
miles ahead on the interstate."

"Frank, mind your manners," Iris scolded gently. "There's no sense in them standing out in this damp, muggy weather after everything they've been through." She stepped in front of her husband and opened the screen door wide in a friendly small-town welcome. "Come on in, and we'll see what we can do to get you back on the road and safely to your family."

Dean inclined his head gratefully. "Thank you, ma'am, we really do appreciate that."

"Yes, thank you," Jo said, and followed Dean inside the small but cozy house.

The rich, redolent scent of hearty meat and vegetables curled around them, along with something sweeter, like baked apples and cinnamon. Not surprisingly, Dean's stomach growled loudly, obnoxiously, making Jo bite back laughter and Dean extend an apology for his rumbling belly.

Iris's eyes widened at the ravenous sound, though she waved away Dean's embarrassment. "There's absolutely nothing to apologize for. You must be starved after waiting out the storm then walking to our place. Let's get the two of you fed."

"Oh, no, really, that's not necessary," Jo insisted, certain she felt the very hungry man standing beside her squeeze her hand in protest.

"There's plenty, and we insist, don't we Frank?" Iris didn't give the other man a chance to answer. "What with living out in the country and no neighbors nearby and my children scattered about the state with their own families, it's not very often that we get company. And it would make me feel so much better knowing that you two left here with full stomachs.''

"Then we'd love to join you for supper," Dean said eagerly before Jo could refuse again.

"Wonderful." Iris beamed happily. "You two have a seat in the dining room right in there. Frank, you come help me put everything in serving dishes and bring it out to the table."

The older couple disappeared into the kitchen and Dean led the way into an adjoining room where they sat next to each other at two of the six chairs at the oak table. Jo turned to Dean and took the opportunity alone to express her disbelief over his fabrication of their relationship.

"Your *wife?*" she whispered incredulously as they waited for their hosts to return. "What was *that* all about?"

He blinked guilelessly. "Would you rather I told our only source of help that you'd taken me into custody believing I was a felon waiting to stand trial for grand theft auto and that you're taking me back to San Francisco to clear my name?"

She swallowed laughter at his matter-of-fact tone and acceded to his point. "No, I guess not. But acting like a married couple is a bit extreme, don't you think?"

"What can it hurt?" He shrugged lazily and brought the back of her hand to his warm lips for a kiss—for show should their hosts be watching, or out of genuine affection, she wasn't sure. Either way it felt good and she enjoyed the attention. "Frank was leery enough of us showing up on his doorstep, and it probably put them at ease and gained their sympathy for our situation, so why not?"

She sighed as he let go of her hand, unable to argue with his logic. "And you get a free meal out of the deal."

"Which you nearly sabotaged," he said, sending her a mock disgruntled glance. "After the physical exertion you put me through this afternoon, I need sustenance. And whatever Iris is cooking smells so much better than the fast food you've been feeding me."

She wrinkled her nose at him, not the least bit insulted by his complaint. "Poor baby. Enjoy supper, and don't expect any gourmet meals when we get to Oakland, either, because it won't happen."

He looked disappointed. "You don't cook?"

"I can microwave a frozen meal really well." Picking up the paper napkin at her place setting, she spread it on her lap. "I learned that particular talent from Cole and Noah when I was about ten."

"That's certainly not a skill to be proud of," he teased. "Even *I* can do better than frozen dinners."

"Quick and easy is my motto. I don't have the time for anything more."

He draped his arm along the back of her chair and leaned close so that it appeared they were having an intimate conversation. "I'm thinking you spend way too much time on the go chasing bad guys and not enough time giving slow and thorough a try."

Were they talking about cooking, sex, or nurturing a relationship? She wasn't certain, but either way she bristled at the insinuation that her job and choice of lifestyle were affecting any of the three, no matter how much it might be true. "It's all by choice. *My* choice," she clarified.

The defensive note in Jo's voice caught Dean off guard. He held her gaze, which glimmered with too much stubborn pride. The woman was way too sensitive about her occupation and the need to defend what she did for a living. He'd only meant that she might try and open herself to other possibilities, ones that might include more than their brief time together, but he lost the opportunity to explain when Frank and Iris entered the dining room carrying platters of fragrant food.

Minutes later, Dean was digging into a plate filled with tender pot roast, potatoes, buttered vegetables that no doubt had been homegrown, and fresh buttermilk biscuits. His moans of appreciation and verbal compliments made Iris blush, though it was obvious that she enjoyed his praise.

Iris poured more iced tea into her glass and refilled her husband's. "Be sure to save room for apple cobbler."

"Not a problem there," Jo said, casting Dean a sweet smile that contradicted the playful provocation he saw in the depths of her eyes. "My *husband* is like a bottomless pit when it comes to food."

"There's nothing wrong with a man having a

healthy appetite,'' Iris said, defending Dean's voracious hunger.

Dean bestowed one of his most charming smiles on his hostess. ''I just don't get meals like this very often at home,'' he said truthfully, though his statement also served to goad Jo, his *wife,* right back. ''So it's a real treat for me when I do.''

''Consider this an open invitation to stop by anytime you're passing through to visit family.'' Iris broke open a biscuit and slathered butter on one steaming half. ''Now tell me, how long have the two of you been married?''

''Just a few months,'' he replied, not missing a beat.

''I knew it!'' Iris glanced excitedly at Frank, who was busy concentrating on his meal. ''Didn't I tell you that these two still had that newlywed glow about them?''

A small smile quirked the older man's mouth, softening the harsher lines etching his features. ''Yep, you certainly did.''

''Oh, to be young and in love and to experience the bliss of being newly married again.'' Iris placed a hand over her heart and sighed dreamily, obviously remembering those early days with Frank. ''Though our first year together was the best in so many ways, I do have to admit that it was also the toughest.''

''In what way?'' Jo asked as she pushed her fork through her vegetables, her tone curious. ''That is, if you don't mind me asking.''

''Not at all.'' Iris dabbed her mouth with her napkin, warming to the subject. "My Frank has always been the strong, silent type and a man of few words. He prefers to think of it as being contemplative, but a good amount of it is due to sheer stubbornness, I've come to learn—and accept."

Frank *hrmph'd* in response as he ate a bite of roast, but didn't deny her claim.

She placed a hand on her husband's arm in a loving, soothing gesture. "We didn't have much when we first married, and times were certainly very lean. Through the hardships we had many disagreements, and one of the most important lessons we learned was that in order for us to make our marriage last and be happy together we had to compromise on certain issues. Give and take equally, and find a common ground."

Her words struck a chord in Dean, one that made him realize that compromise had been one of the essential ingredients missing from his own parents' marriage. "That's very sound advice."

Iris smiled gently. "It's made a huge difference in our relationship, and has carried us through forty-three happy years of marriage."

"Forty-three years," Jo said, her tone soft and wistful. "That's wonderful."

"We think so," Iris said, speaking for both her and her husband. "And don't forget to make sure you both take time in your busy lives for each other, to keep the romance in your marriage fresh and exciting."

Dean set his fork on his empty plate and pushed it

aside. "We'll be sure to do that," he said, wishing his own parents had had someone like Iris to offer them that particular piece of advice somewhere along the way. Not that his father would have made the time easily, but possibly their marriage would have been much different if his mother had insisted on more attention, and his father had compromised even half-way.

Frank took a long drink of his iced tea, then swiped his napkin across his mouth, done with his supper. "I think the boy here is ready for some of your apple cobbler, Iris."

Dean recognized a switch in topic when he heard one, and apparently so did Iris, who said no more on the subject of love and marriage. "I'd love some cobbler," he replied, unable to pass up such a delicious treat.

"I'll clear the table while you serve up dessert," Jo offered. Standing, she stacked their dirty dishes then followed Iris into an adjoining room.

While the two women were in the kitchen, Dean addressed the problem of Jo's Suburban being stranded. "Do you know of a local towing service I could call?"

"No need to call anyone," Frank said, shaking his head. "I have a towing hitch on my truck and I'll take the two of you and your vehicle into Medford."

"You really don't have to do that."

Frank's brows rose comically. "After everything you just heard during supper, do you really think that

Iris would let me get any peace if I didn't see you two newlyweds safely into town myself?''

Dean laughed at the other man's dry sense of humor that held so much truth. "No, I suppose not. Thank you. You both have been very kind and hospitable considering you weren't exactly expecting company.''

"I should be thanking you.'' Frank leaned back in his chair, a hint of a smile making an appearance. "I think you made Iris's evening, and I'll reap the benefits.'' He followed that up with a sly wink.

The four of them spent the next half hour enjoying warmed apple cobbler with French vanilla ice cream and light, friendly conversation. Too soon it was time to leave, and Iris insisted on sending them off with a care package of leftovers should Dean get hungry later that night, which Jo assured the other woman was a definite possibility. After a round of warm hugs from Iris, she pressed a piece of paper into Dean's hand with their phone number and extended an invitation to stop by anytime.

With one last wave, Dean climbed into Frank's truck next to Jo, his *wife,* and wondered if he was the only one feeling an indescribable tug of longing after their visit with Iris and Frank, the only one coveting the special relationship the older couple shared.

He sighed. Considering Jo's practical, independent views when it came to men and relationships, probably so.

10

THEY DROPPED THE SUBURBAN OFF at a service station in Medford to be repaired first thing the following morning. By the time they'd checked into a motel one block over, another thunderstorm had moved in. Leaving the registration office, Jo and Dean hightailed it to their assigned room just as another downpour hit, dampening their hair and clothes all over again.

Laughing at their bad luck, Jo closed the heavy metal door, locked the bolt, and put Dean's wrapped package of food on the small table in the corner for him to feast on later. He dropped their bags at the far end of the king-sized bed and turned to her with the same private grin he'd been wearing since leaving Iris and Frank's place.

They were alone, spending yet another night together, and her belly fluttered with renewed awareness. "What are you smiling at, *husband?*" she teased as she unclipped her cell phone from the waistband of her jeans. Finally, a signal, and three voice mail messages waiting for her, she noticed. No doubt Cole had tried to contact her. She needed to call her brother to give him an update on her whereabouts and

Dean's innocence. She wasn't looking forward to their conversation.

Dean's shoulders rolled in a lazy shrug. "I just keep thinking about Iris and her matrimonial lecture."

"Her advice seems to have worked well for her and Frank for the past forty-three years. You don't see relationships like theirs very often," she said, remembering too well her own mother and father's inability to compromise and work through their problems. Setting her phone on the dresser until she had a few moments alone, she tipped her head curiously at Dean. "Were your parents like Frank and Iris before your dad died?"

He sat on the edge of the mattress, clearly hesitating before answering. "Unfortunately, no. My parents remained married up to the day my father died, but for as long as I can remember, their relationship was strained."

Intrigued, she leaned her bottom against the dresser and propped her hands on either side of her hips. "Do you know why things were strained?"

He untied his shoelaces and tugged off a shoe, a damp sock, then worked on the other pair. "Mainly because Colter Traffic Control was my father's mistress. He spent just about every waking hour at the business, leaving me and my mother alone for the most part. In a lot of ways, he was like a stranger to us. Then again, I can't ever remember my mother insisting that my father spend more time with us. She just accepted things for what they were, though there was no doubt she resented how much time he devoted to the business." He combed his fingers through his thick, dark hair, dragging the unruly strands away from his face. "Hell, even as a kid *I* resented my father being a workaholic and not showing up at my softball games, or missing an important event or holiday, and not getting home until after midnight most weekdays."

She listened to his story and applied it to her own parents' rocky marriage. Different circumstances, but the end result had been a couple who'd drifted far, far apart, just as Dean's parents had. "Don't you think your mother and father were equally at fault for their relationship deteriorating?"

"Oh, most definitely. My mother should have insisted on more quality time, and my father should have been more aware of his family's needs. But he was so caught up in the fear of being poor like his own father had left his family when he'd split on them that he couldn't see past the driving need to *work,* no matter the cost to me and my mother." His gaze met hers, filled with emotions she couldn't fully decipher. "And would you believe that *my* biggest fear is that I'm going to end up just like my father. Sounds like a vicious cycle, doesn't it?"

From what she'd learned about his dad, and from what she'd seen firsthand with Dean, she couldn't envision this sensitive, ethical man in front of her forsaking a wife and family—for any reason. "I can't see that happening, not when you're taking steps to make sure your life ends up differently than your father's."

''It *did* happen, Jo.'' He scrubbed a hand down his face, which did nothing to wipe away the regret etching his features. ''I led a relatively carefree life before taking over the company. I went out with friends, had a good time, and was even a bit of a rebel. I might have been sucked into the business out of pressure and guilt, but I lost a fiancée because I wasn't able to make room for a relationship along with the demands of the company.''

Her chest expanded with startled shock. He'd been engaged. Oh, wow. The news hit her in her midsection and made her experience a twisting bit of jealousy toward the woman who had once been this man's significant other. The sensation threw her off-kilter because it was such an unfamiliar emotion when it came to men. And she had no business experiencing it with Dean, who was only in her life temporarily.

''Maybe it just wasn't the right time for you to settle down and get married,'' she said, more reasonably than she felt.

''Maybe not, but looking back, no matter how I sum things up, I was more like my father than I cared to admit.'' He exhaled hard, as if trying to release some of the self-condemnation bogging him down. ''I sacrificed a woman I cared a great deal about for a business that consumed me as much as it had my father. I've spent the past three years solely focused on work, to the exclusion of all else. I want part of my old life back, and now I'm determined to make changes that suit *me*.''

Her fingers curled tight over the edge of the dresser. "You deserve that."

"We all deserve to be true to ourselves." He stared her straight in the eyes, connecting with her in a way that pulled at deeply buried emotions. "Don't you think so, Jo?"

She swallowed the tight knot that suddenly formed in her throat, feeling as though his question was dealing with the two of them directly. "Yes, I believe everyone deserves that chance."

But other than working on her abduction cases, she didn't know what she wanted out of life, was ultimately afraid of taking risks that meant openly putting her emotions on the line and possibly losing an integral part of her soul in the process, as she had with her partner, Brian. He'd been the only man who'd believed in equality amongst colleagues, and never once coddled her out in the field. He'd had faith in her abilities as a female cop, had become one of her most trusted friends, and had given Jo the confidence to believe in herself...until the night her courage had been put to the test and Brian had paid with his life.

Her chest expanded with the dull, familiar ache of pain and loss. That kind of emotional sacrifice she never wanted to experience again. And knowing that, could she ever be true to herself as Dean was asking? It was a tough question considering she no longer trusted her feelings on an intimate or personal level. She found it easier, safer, to maintain her carefully controlled existence and not let anyone close enough to see her own doubts, the guilt she carried, and the vulnerability she hid behind a durable and resistant facade.

A clap of thunder rumbled in the distance as a long silence descended between them. Finally, when it was obvious that there was nothing left to say, Dean stood and peeled off his wet T-shirt, then went to work on the button and zipper of his jeans.

"I'm going to go take a long, hot shower," he said, pushing the denim down his muscular legs and stepping out of them.

Jo's mind went on sensory overload, and her breath whooshed out of her lungs. After their tryst in the truck he hadn't put on any briefs beneath his pants. Now he stood before her, magnificently naked except for a lazy, all-male smile gracing his lips. He was completely at ease with his nudity, as well he should be, considering what a gorgeous, made-for-sex-and-sin body he possessed.

She lifted her gaze back to safer territory—his face. Though he hadn't outright asked her to join him in the shower, the invitation in his bright green eyes was unmistakable. He wanted her to come with him, but he was leaving the final decision up to her, seemingly not wanting to push for more than she was willing or ready to give.

She appreciated his insight, his sensitivity, because she had no idea where her boundaries with this man lay anymore. And that realization frightened her. Her mind was filled with confusion, her heart playing tug-of-war with emotions she'd never intended to allow into her affair with Dean. What had begun as satiating mutual desires had somehow, some way grown into a bittersweet longing that threatened all those barriers she'd erected after Brian's death.

Knowing just how close she was to ditching the business call to her brother in lieu of pleasure with Dean, she picked up her cell phone and held the unit in her palm like a lifeline. "I, um, need to call Cole and let him know what's going on."

He nodded, accepting her excuse gracefully and seemingly sensing her need for privacy during her conversation with her brother. "If you need me for anything, you know where to find me." He winked at her.

She bit her bottom lip as she watched him walk to the bathroom with his shaving bag in hand. She admired his backside, from his wide shoulders and smooth back, all the way down to a world-class butt that was toned and defined and breathtakingly sexy. He disappeared into the adjoining room, and seconds later the shower turned on.

Banishing the provocative images forming in her mind and knowing where they could lead if she allowed her fantasies to take flight, she checked her voice-mail messages. All three were, indeed, from Cole, and she winced at his brusque tone. He sounded none too pleased that he wasn't able to contact her, and told her to get in touch with him on his cell phone as soon as she retrieved his call. Using her speed dial, she punched in Cole's number, and he picked up on the first ring.

"Sommers here," he said, his voice deep and gruff and highly irritable.

Here we go, she thought. "Cole, it's Jo."

"It's about goddamn time!" he bellowed, loud enough that she had to hold the unit away from her ear. "Do you realize that you should have been home by now, and that I've been worried thinking the worst—"

"The Suburban broke down outside of Medford and I've been without a cell phone connection," she interrupted his tirade, knowing from experience just how long-winded her brother could be with his lectures if she let him. "I finally got the truck towed to a service station, but the blown radiator hose can't be fixed until the morning."

He grew quiet as he digested what she told him, which only heightened Jo's anxiety of what was to come. "Do you have Dean Colter with you?"

"Yeah, I've got him." She tugged the elastic band from her hair and massaged her fingers along her tight scalp. "I picked him up at his residence in Seattle, exactly where you traced him to."

"Is he giving you a hard time?"

Well, now, that all depended on how she interpreted the word "hard," she thought with a bit of private humor she knew her brother wouldn't appreciate. "No, he's fine, Cole, and not any trouble at all. And I'm fine, too."

"I'll head out to Medford," he said, obviously choosing not to believe her and exerting too much of that overprotectiveness she resented when it came to her doing a job. "I can be there in a few hours—"

"Cole, I can handle it. This isn't my first recovery case, so stop treating me like a novice." Annoyance vibrated through her and spilled into her voice. Knowing she had to tell him the truth about Dean sooner or later, she opted to get the discussion over with now. "Besides, Dean Colter is an innocent man."

"What the hell are you talking about?" he barked into the phone.

Cringing, she sat down on the edge of the bed and rubbed the sharp ache starting to throb in her temples. "You need to call Vince and tell him that he's after the wrong guy. The felon he's looking for isn't Dean Colter, and the real culprit is out running free."

"Goddamn it, Jo, are you nuts?" His clipped tone clearly implied that she was off her rocker. "Do you or do you not have Dean Colter in custody?" he asked succinctly.

"Yes, I do," she replied calmly. "But this is a case of mistaken identity."

"Is that what he's convinced you to believe?" Cole snorted derisively. "That's the oldest trick in the book, and if you so much as fall for that line this will be the last recovery case I ever send you on."

She bristled defensively, hating her brother's inability to trust in her. "I believe him, Cole," she said, willing to put her own reputation and sanity on the line for a man who should have been long gone after cuffing her to his bed last night, but had remained behind to convince her of his innocence. "And before you blow a gasket, at least listen to me. Dean Colter, the *real* Dean Colter, had his briefcase and wallet stolen on a recent trip to San Francisco. His social security card, credit cards, his driver's license—the same driver's license Vince has on file for him—all of them were taken. The guy that was arrested might look like Dean Colter with dark hair and green eyes and similar features, but he assumed his identity."

"You don't know that for certain," he shot back. "And it's not up to you to determine his innocence. Get his ass back here ASAP so we can get him fingerprinted and verified."

"I intend to do just that."

"Good. Keep him cuffed at all times..." Cole's voice trailed off as a sudden realization struck. "Jesus, you do have him restrained, don't you?"

Her pause in answering was enough for Cole to come to his own conclusions. She couldn't and wouldn't lie to her brother, but neither was she about to explain how Dean had managed to get his handcuffs off...how he had transferred them to her wrists and secured her to his bed...how her dreamlike state would have made her vulnerable to a man less honorable than Dean had been. But that incident had ultimately led to proof of his innocence, not that she'd ever expect Cole to understand her reasons for believing and trusting in Dean. And her brother certainly wouldn't condone just how far she'd allowed things to go with a man whose name was linked with grand theft auto.

Cole's colorful curse broke through her thoughts and jolted her back to the present. "You're not thinking straight, Jo, and you're going to do something stupid if you haven't already. Or worse, go and get yourself hurt or killed just like Brian."

Her whole body jerked at his verbal slap. The sting of his words rippled through her and made her stomach cramp. Cole doubted her ability to make level-headed decisions, to decipher right from wrong, and while a part of her couldn't blame him for letting her past actions speak for themselves, she had to wonder if she'd ever get past the stigma that had haunted her for the past two years. Weakness. Incompetence. A sense of failure. Would everyone forever question her credibility and mental stability when it came to risky situations? The guilt of the past was hers to bear, but what did she have to do to absolve herself of all the doubts that colored everyone's opinion of her?

She inhaled a steadying breath. "Your confidence in me is overwhelming."

"Dammit, Jo, I didn't mean it like that," he said, his tone holding nuances of contrition, but the damage had already been done. "I worry about you, and I think this guy is trying to snow you."

And, bottom line, Cole didn't think she could handle the situation or Dean. "Think whatever you'd like," she said, her voice cool. "He's given me every reason to believe him. I even found a new driver's license and credit cards that corroborated his story."

"There's ten thousand dollars riding on this guy, Jo," he said, ignoring her attempt to sway him to her way of thinking. "Don't blow it for me, you, or Vince."

"You can't claim bond on an innocent man," she snapped, her temper getting the best of her.

"You can't know that until we have proof," he returned just as testily. "What the hell is going on with you, Jo?"

"Nothing I'm not grown up enough to handle." Too late, she'd revealed way more than she'd intended. "Call Vince, make him aware of the situation, and if all goes well with getting the Suburban repaired, I'll see you at the office sometime tomorrow." She disconnected the line before her brother could say anything more, and went one step further and shut down her cell phone so he couldn't call her back tonight.

Standing, she set the phone on the dresser, feeling frustrated and mentally drained. And no matter how she tried to block her brother's doubts from her mind, she couldn't stop Cole's harsh words from echoing in her head, over and over... *You're not thinking straight, Jo, and you're going to do something stupid if you haven't already.*

She knew her brother was referring to something dangerous and life-threatening as far as her "prisoner" was concerned, but she realized that the only thing in jeopardy in relation to Dean was her heart. In a short amount of time he'd shaken up the very guarded life in which she'd lived the past two years. Yet, despite the emotional threat Dean posed, despite knowing that each encounter with him pulled her in deeper and deeper, he drew her even now in a way she couldn't ignore.

The need she'd developed for Dean was strong, scary, but undeniable. Wanting to forget her brother's lecture and all the turmoil that awaited her back in San Francisco, and aching to savor this last night with Dean and the mindless pleasure he gave her, she gave in to the sensual cravings and deepest desires he evoked. One more memory to make and cherish before Dean claimed his life back and they went their separate ways.

Stripping out of her clothes, she entered the bathroom and opened the glass enclosure where Dean was soaping up his chest and arms. Steam billowed around her, kissing the tips of her taut breasts, dampening her skin, and heating her just as much as his appreciative gaze that consumed her in one sweeping glance.

She touched a hand to the sheen of moisture gathering between her breasts and followed the trail to her belly, marveling at the fact that she didn't possess an ounce of modesty or inhibition with this highly sexual man. Amazed, too, that she could enthrall him as much as he excited her. And for the moment, for tonight, that's all that mattered.

"Mind if I join you?" she asked softly.

A wicked grin curved his mouth. "Sure. I could use someone to scrub my back and all those other hard-to-reach places."

She smiled in return, already feeling her spirits lift

and the last bit of her conversation with Cole fade away. "Only if you'll scrub mine, too."

"Now that would be my pleasure," he drawled, and moved back to make room for her in the small cubicle.

She stepped into the shower and closed the glass door, cocooning them in steam and moisture and heat. Lots of heat. He reached out and tucked his finger beneath her chin, lifting her face so she was staring into his compelling eyes that seemed to search deep into her soul and see vulnerable emotions she tried so hard to hide from everyone else.

"Hey, you okay?" he murmured.

The man was so in tune to her shifting feelings, so concerned about her welfare, despite how much he wanted her. "Yeah, I'm just fine," she assured him, and took the soapy washcloth from his hand. "Now turn around so I can scrub your back."

He hesitated a moment, then did as she ordered. She swept the terry cloth across his broad shoulders, and took her time washing the slope of his spine, his hips, buttocks and thighs. Warm water drizzled over them, rinsing away the soapy suds and leaving his skin smooth and slick to the touch.

And touch him, she did. Letting the washcloth drop to the tiled floor, she slipped her hands around to his chest and skimmed her palms down to his abdomen while lapping the moisture from his neck with her tongue. Standing on tiptoes, she deliberately pressed her wet breasts along his back, her feminine mound to his buttocks, and rubbed sinuously against him as she trailed her lips along his jaw. With a low, needy moan, he turned his head, his mouth seeking hers, but she continued to tease him with soft, fleeting kisses as her fingers delved through dense curls and wrapped around the hard, straining length of his erection.

He instinctively bucked his hips, sliding his shaft more snugly into her grip, and she squeezed him tight and brushed her thumb over the silky, pulsing head of his penis. He sucked in a harsh breath and grabbed her wrist before she could increase the exquisite friction and send him over the edge.

In one fluid motion he managed to turn them both around, so that he was standing behind her now, and flattened her hands on the wall in front of her. She turned her face away from the shower spray drenching her, and he pushed the spigot downward, so the stream of water cascaded over her breasts, licked across her belly, caressed the length of her legs and trickled along the tender flesh in between her thighs like the soft, delicate lap of his tongue. Her provocative thoughts mingled with erotic sensation, heightening her awareness and making her entire body swell with shameless anticipation.

Holding her hands in place on the wall, he insinuated his bare foot and knee between her legs and widened her stance even more. "Have *you* ever been frisked before, Jo?"

A shiver of excitement coursed through her, adding to the chaotic rush of water over her sensitized skin. Professionally, during training, yes, she'd been patted down, but never, ever by a man who turned her on and set her senses on fire with a hunger and desire she couldn't seem to control.

"Not like this," she whispered, wanting this, wanting him.

"It's a standard search, Ms. Sommers," he drawled into her ear, his amusing words reminiscent of the same ones she'd spoken to him when she'd taken him into custody. "Just to be sure you aren't carrying any concealed weapons."

She laughed huskily, then groaned as his hands slid down her wet arms, cupped her breasts in his palms and his thumbs flicked over her nipples in a tantalizing caress. Flirtatious and teasing, he skimmed his fingers over her curves, along her sleek skin, down the length of her body, slowly, sensuously, bringing nerve endings alive with desire. It didn't escape her notice that he was once again holding the reins of this seduction, controlling her every response and ultimate surrender, yet she was too aroused, too needy, to care.

"Ummm, only one more place to check," he said, and straightened, bringing their bodies flush, his chest to her back, his groin to her bottom, where his thick erection nestled provocatively. He slipped a hand around to her belly, coasted lower, and parted her swollen, aching flesh with long fingers. She moaned. His first probing touch felt so hot, so acute...and she felt so sensitive, so wet—ready and primed for a wild, uninhibited orgasm.

"Oh, yeah," he encouraged in a low growl against her neck. "Come for me, Joelle, just like this..."

With skillful, knowing strokes—the same strokes

she'd taught him that afternoon in the truck—he turned her body to liquid, her mind to mush, and pushed her to the very edge of ecstasy. The pressure and tension spiraled to an exquisite pitch, and then she was falling and crying out and shuddering as pure, carnal pleasure shook her to the very core of her being.

She gulped air into her lungs, and her quivering legs buckled. He caught her around the waist, holding her up, keeping her safe in the shelter of his arms, then turned her around in his embrace. Dark, glittering eyes met hers, and he pressed her up against the stall while lukewarm water showered down upon them. He crushed his lips to hers, parting them easily, and kissed her long, deep and hard as the entire length of his body moved restlessly against hers. Their wet skin rubbed, igniting a fire deep within.

Needing more, Jo wrenched her mouth from Dean's as a feverish sound escaped her throat, as did the softest of pleas. "Dean, I want you inside me. Please."

"I'm there," he promised, and tucked his hands beneath her bottom, spreading her knees wide as he lifted her feet off the ground. Wedging his thighs in between hers, he pulled her supple, giving body back down to his and buried his rigid erection to the hilt.

A searing heat shimmered through her and a startled gasp ripped from her chest. Her shoulders were braced against the wall for leverage, and she automatically wrapped her arms around his neck and clenched her legs tight around his hips to help hold on.

"Oh, God, are you sure about this position?" she asked breathlessly, so incredibly aroused she knew she wouldn't last long, even this second time.

"Oh, yeah, I'm very sure," he whispered in her ear, his words confident, his breath hot. "There's something to be said for being a featherweight. All you have to do is hang on, sweetheart, and enjoy the ride."

With a strength and agility that amazed her, he gripped her hips in his large, strong hands and worked her body precisely the way he wanted, exactly the way she craved. He surged deep inside her, withdrew, slid upward once more, pushing into her, over and over. He felt so vibrant, so alive, like a flame burning inside her, consuming her. She clung to him as he increased the rhythm of his thrusts, as he sank deeper into her soft, welcoming body.

And still, it wasn't enough.

Wet, slippery skin created an unbearable friction, and she tangled her fingers in his wet, silky hair as she arched into him with every thrust, fusing them more intimately. His harsh breathing quickened against her throat as his hips pushed more forcefully against her, pumping harder, faster. A frenzied need built, sizzling hot and immediate. Demanding in its intensity.

Pleasure swelled to a bursting point then exploded, dragging them both under at the same time. He caught her moans of ecstasy with his mouth as the pulsing spasms shaking his body rippled into hers.

Boneless and sated, he eased her down the wall until he was kneeling on the tiled floor with her straddling his waist and their bodies still joined. His heartbeat thundered against her chest, and she relished the connection, the quiet, perfect intimacy of the moment.

Cool water cascaded over them, chasing away the heat that had scorched them both. She brushed a kiss to his full, soft lips and pressed her forehead against his. "It seems *you're* the only one with a concealed weapon," she teased.

He grinned lazily. "At least I know what to do with it."

She chuckled at his sexy reply. "Oh, that you do, Mr. Colter."

His gaze turned a deep, serious shade of jade that was underscored with a wealth of tenderness—the kind she'd had very little of in her lifetime. "I think I'm addicted to you, Jo Sommers."

She swallowed hard, fearing the same thing, that this man was quickly becoming a habit she didn't want to shake. And she had no idea what she was going to do about the growing obsession.

11

AFTER A NIGHT of intense pleasure and incredible, erotic passion, Dean was disappointed, but not entirely surprised, that Jo had woken that morning with her emotions withdrawn and tucked neatly away, and her demeanor all business and much too formal. They'd eaten breakfast at a local diner, then walked the one block to the service station to wait for the Suburban to be repaired. Since hitting the road hours ago, she'd adeptly avoided any deep, serious conversation that might lead to something more personal—such as their current relationship and what lay ahead for them…if anything at all.

Gone was the teasing between them. And gone was the warm and willing woman who'd allowed him free, uninhibited access to her body and desires, to be replaced by a contemplative and quiet young lady who seemed to disregard all the intimacies that they'd shared the past two days. And the closer they got to their destination, the more emotional distance each mile seemed to put between him and Jo.

Shifting restlessly in his car seat, Dean exhaled a low, heavy breath. Despite his frustration, he kept his concentration on the stretch of freeway Jo was navigating toward San Francisco, his gaze off the silent woman sitting beside him, and his thoughts to himself. The latter was the most difficult since there was so much he wanted to say to her, so many uncertainties he wanted to talk about in terms of them, together.

In a very short amount of time he'd grown to care for Jo in ways he'd never anticipated. Hell, he knew his feelings for her went deeper than just fondness and affection and sexual desire, encompassing emotions and needs that made his head spin and his heart pump hard in his chest. He wasn't willing to walk away from her with nothing more than a friendly goodbye once his name was cleared, yet she'd never indicated she wanted anything more than a brief fling. He also knew he had no right to ask her for something more long-term when he had to get his own life in order.

In the meantime, no matter how difficult, he'd respect the personal boundaries Jo had erected since this morning, even though he hated being shut out in the process. If he'd learned one thing about this stubborn, self-sufficient woman, he knew she needed her space and didn't appreciate being pressured, coddled, or backed into a corner with ultimatums.

By the time they finally pulled up to a one-story brick building with the company name Sommers Investigative Specialists etched on the front door, the tension surrounding Jo and in the truck was nearly palpable. The emotional distance between them was as wide as the Golden Gate Bridge he'd glimpsed on the way to her brother's offices.

She cut the engine, allowed a deep sigh to unravel out of her, then glanced his way. "Well, here we are. One step closer to you being a free man."

He chuckled, trying to lighten the moment between them. "I never thought I'd love hearing the sound of that."

The faint smile he'd managed to glean faltered and shifted into a more serious expression. "Dean...I know you're innocent but, just so you know, Cole isn't too thrilled that you aren't cuffed and restrained, despite what I think or feel."

The realization that she'd defended him to her brother pleased him immensely. "You told him I'm innocent?"

She nodded and rubbed her palms down her jean-clad thighs. "Yeah, last night when I called him. I tried to explain about your last visit to San Francisco and someone stealing your ID and assuming your identity, but he was skeptical."

Skeptical of not only him as a runaway felon, but also of Jo's decision to leave him free and unbound, he realized. Her admission of that fact had obviously cost her a good chunk of trust and respect from her brother. Reaching across the distance separating them, he gently brushed his fingertips along her cheek and threaded them through her silky hair. He needed that connection with her before they walked into the office, met with her brother, and everything between them shifted and changed even more.

"Thank you, Jo," he said, his voice low and rich with meaning.

A small frown marred her brows. "For what?"

He smiled, wishing he had a direct link to what was going on in that head of hers. Then again, maybe he was better off not knowing. "For believing in me." Cupping the back of her head in his palm, he drew her mouth to his and kissed her softly, letting his lips linger on hers so he could savor her sweet taste.

She was the first to pull back, her reluctance to go further, to give more, tangible—as was the resistance she struggled to maintain with him. He stared into her eyes, saw a deeper longing that contradicted all her attempts to remain detached, and knew in that moment that somehow, some way, he had to find a way to convince her that he believed in her, too.

WITH A DEEP BREATH for fortitude, Jo pushed open the glass door leading into the reception area of Sommers Investigative Specialists and stepped inside, with Dean close behind. As soon as she met Melodie's apologetic gaze from across the room, she knew the confrontation to come with her brother wasn't going to be an easy one.

The receptionist punched the intercom button on the phone to her right, her gaze drifting to Dean with unabashed curiosity. "Cole, Jo's back."

Jo stopped in front of Melodie's desk, unable to blame the younger woman for doing her job, and knowing without a shadow of doubt that Cole had instructed his secretary to inform him immediately upon Jo's arrival. "I'm surprised the fire-breathing dragon wasn't standing guard at the front door," she said wryly.

Melodie smothered a grin. "He's definitely been agitated all morning. Thank God Noah showed up about a half hour ago to turn in his surveillance report on the Blythes' divorce case—it's kept both of them in Cole's office and out of my hair. Before that, he was pacing through the reception area and driving me nuts."

Seconds later, Cole and Noah emerged from the hallway leading to their individual offices. Cole rushed forward, his stride swift with purpose, while Noah, the more lax of the two, hung back and let their older sibling take charge, as always. While Cole was aggressive in business and even in personal matters, Noah wasn't one to dive into a predicament without first analyzing the situation from every possible angle.

Jo wasn't sure which brother she found more unnerving at the moment, considering they were both dissecting Dean in completely opposite ways—Cole with open distrust, and Noah with reserved scrutiny and interest. And then there was Dean, who stood calmly beside her, the tips of his fingers casually pushed into the pockets of his jeans and his stance and expression relaxed. He took Cole's blatant suspicion in stride, possibly because she'd warned him of her brother's attitude up-front. At any rate, Dean's cool, unruffled composure made her want to grin because it seemed to annoy Cole even more.

No introductions were necessary, and since Cole didn't seem inclined to partake of a friendly handshake with Dean, Jo didn't bother with pleasantries. "Did you call Vince?"

Cole unclenched his tight jaw. "Yeah, I called him," he replied gruffly, and transferred his dark blue gaze back to her. "He finds your story just as hard to believe as I do."

She lifted her chin a few notches, wondering how she'd been so unfortunate as to end up with all the short genes when both of her brothers were over six feet tall. "Then it's a matter of taking Dean in, getting him fingerprinted, and verifying his credibility."

Cole crossed his arms over his broad chest, his gaze narrowing on Dean. "Yeah, I guess so."

As if sensing the growing tension between brother and sister and accused felon, Noah stepped forward. "I'll take him down to the precinct and handle the paperwork to clear his name."

Cole and Noah had been protecting and sheltering her for so long that it was an automatic reaction for them to step in and take over, despite that Dean was her skip and her responsibility. For once, Jo didn't put up an argument. She didn't have the energy to spar with either brother, nor did she want to make a scene in front of Dean.

Besides, if she was honest with herself, a part of her was grateful for the reprieve. She needed distance and time away from Dean, to gather her wits and put things back in proper perspective—mentally and emotionally.

"I'm Noah Sommers," her brother introduced himself. He extended his hand toward the man standing patiently beside her, and Jo appreciated the display of trust Noah, at least, was offering on her behalf.

"Dean Colter." A half grin canted Dean's lips as he accepted Noah's amicable gesture. "But then you already knew that."

A dark brow lifted in amusement. "But which Dean Colter are you really?" Noah asked, openly joking about his claim of mistaken identity.

Dean chuckled, completely at ease with the situation. "We'll find out soon enough, now won't we?"

"We certainly will." Noah withdrew his car keys from his front pocket and cast Jo and Cole a quick glance. "We'll be back in a few hours."

Noah headed for the front door, but Dean didn't immediately follow. Instead, he turned toward her, his gaze seeking and finding hers. The silence that suddenly descended over the room as everyone waited to hear what he had to say to her was deafening.

"I'll see you later?" he asked, his tone low and intimate and filled with expectation.

A blush swept across her cheeks, and Jo hated that everyone was privy to that telltale sign. "Sure," she said, striving for a nonchalance to counteract the flush of awareness heating her skin. She'd see him one last time—to drive him to the airport and send him back to Washington before she fell any harder or deeper for him.

With that promise from her, Dean was out the door and gone, leaving her to deal with Cole's brooding silence as he stormed off toward his office, and the eager fascination glimmering in Melodie's eyes. She thought about following her brother and confronting him, but she already knew what he thought and felt— about her and the situation with Dean. He'd made his disapproval abundantly clear, and she knew from past experience there was no reasoning with Cole when his mind was set, so she didn't even try.

She returned to her private office, planning to spend the rest of the afternoon burying her thoughts in outstanding cases awaiting her attention. Unfortunately, her peaceful, solitary break wasn't to be granted. Before she had the opportunity to sit down in the chair behind her desk, Melodie slipped into her office after a quick knock on the door.

"You had a few calls this morning," she said, waving the pink message slips she held in her hand.

"Thank you." Jo accepted the notes and glanced through the messages, penned in Melodie's neat, efficient handwriting. None was urgent or important, thank goodness.

Apparently in no hurry to leave, Melodie settled into one of the chairs in front of Jo's desk and crossed one leg over the other. "Who would have thought that an escaped felon could be sooo sexy and charming."

There was no mistaking who she was referring to. "Dean isn't an escaped felon."

Melodie grinned in satisfaction. "Ahh, that may be true, but you didn't deny that he was sexy and charming."

She shot her friend a direct look. "And your point is?"

"I'm going to ask what no one else in this office has the nerve to," she said, displaying a gutsiness that surprised Jo, since Melodie was normally so reserved. Too bad she couldn't bring herself to use that bold assertiveness on Cole who could use a good dose of his own medicine from his secretary.

Jo shuffled through the paperwork and reports she'd left on her desk last Friday to attend to when she returned to the office. "And what question is that?"

Melodie leaned forward, her eyes alight with anticipation. "Is there something going on between you and Dean?"

"What makes you ask that?" she asked without missing a beat.

"Aww, come on, Jo. *You* might have done a decent job at avoiding the attraction between the two of you out in the reception area, but judging by the intimate way Dean kept on looking at you it was obvious that *something's* going on."

Jo inwardly cringed. If Melodie had seen and sensed the sensual connection between her and Dean, then no doubt so had her brothers. However, she wasn't about to admit to anything.

Melodie continued. "And since I can only dream of my own fantasy man looking at me that way, let me live vicariously through you."

Unbidden, images flashed in her mind, of Dean dragging ice over her breasts and belly and following the cold trail with his heated mouth, his strong body moving over hers, in hers, slow and sure, coaxing her surrender which she'd given him willingly. Numerous times.

Jo shook her head, as much to dismiss Melodie's question as to clear her mind of those provocative and very private scenarios she had no intention of sharing with anyone. "Sorry, but there's nothing to tell."

Melodie regarded her for a few extra seconds. "I think you're holding out on me, but just so you know, I'm here if you need to talk."

Jo said nothing more, and just then the phone rang, saving her from any further response. With one last encouraging smile, Melodie hustled out of her office to take the call at her own desk.

Dropping into her chair with a heavy, soul-deep exhale, Jo leaned back and closed her eyes, forcing herself to relax. Much to her relief, everyone left her alone for the rest of the afternoon to work through her abduction cases on the Internet, until Noah returned with Dean a few hours later.

Saving the document she'd been typing up on her computer, Jo watched as Dean sauntered into her office with an easygoing grin that made her pulse flutter and need coil deep in her belly. No matter how much she wanted to give in to her desires when it came to this earthy, sexual man, she struggled to squash the sensations. She was determined to keep things between them platonic from here on out. Another couple of hours, and he'd be long gone. No sense complicating matters by giving in to the temptation he presented.

"How did it go?" she asked, closing the open file folder in front of her.

"Your brother didn't interrogate me too badly." He winked playfully at her.

She winced, not wanting to know what they'd discussed, especially if it pertained to the two of them and their recent road trip. "I meant how did it go down at the station?"

She expected him to sit down in one of the chairs, but instead he rounded her desk, came to a stop next to her, and perched his hip on the edge of the sturdy walnut surface. "A set of fingerprints proved my identity and that I'm not the guy in the mug shot you showed me. I was cleared of any charges, but unfortunately there's still some guy out there assuming my identity, and until he's caught I'm forced to share my name with a felon."

"I'm sorry," she said, truly feeling bad about that.

"Yeah, the whole situation is frustrating as hell," he agreed.

She inhaled and forced a bright smile. "At least you're now free to head back to Seattle and get back to that vacation I interrupted."

The leg closest to her swung back and forth, brushing against her thigh and stirring up a restlessness she'd thought she'd put a tight rein on. "Actually, I was thinking about sticking around for a few days."

She blinked in surprise. "You were?"

He shrugged casually. "The last time I was in San

Francisco it was all business and I didn't have much time to check out the sights. Besides, I think it would be kinda fun to celebrate my thirty-third birthday on Friday in the city, rather than alone in a cabin out in the middle of nowhere. And before you start worrying, I won't interfere in your work or make demands on your time," he assured her with a charming grin. "In fact, on the way back to the office I had Noah make a stop so I could get a rental car and check into a hotel a few miles away from here."

"Oh." He had everything under control, and he wasn't asking her to spend time with him. She'd wanted the distance and had been the one to establish it, yet she'd never expected to feel a sting of rejection at this unexpected twist in Dean's plans.

He withdrew a slip of paper from his front pocket and put it on the file folder on her desk. "Here's the name and number of the hotel where I'm staying, if you need me for anything," he said, then cast a quick glance at his watch before meeting her gaze again. "I just wanted to let you know what's up with me before I head out for the evening."

Without her. Another stab of envy rippled through her, centering right in the vicinity of her heart. "Where are you off to?"

He stood, looking much too sexy and gorgeous with his tousled hair and form-fitting jeans. Almost good enough for her to think twice about shamelessly begging him to stay with her for the evening, but she refrained from doing so.

"Noah and I seemed to have hit it off," he told her with a smile of amusement. "He said he'd be more than happy to show me the hot spots in San Francisco.''

''Sounds like fun. Have a good time,'' she said, nearly choking on the words and already resenting the time he was going to spend with her carousing, womanizing brother.

''I'm sure we will.'' He headed toward the door, and said over his shoulder, ''I'll stop by sometime tomorrow if I get the chance.'' Then he was gone.

If he got the chance. So casual and indifferent. With a groan, Jo buried her face in her hands and swallowed the tight ache forming in her throat. Severing ties with Dean was exactly what she'd wanted to avoid a deeper involvement, and she'd gotten her wish. So why did she feel so confused and empty inside?

She had no easy answers for the unexpected longings taking up residence in her, but she was very adept at buffeting personal emotions she found difficult to deal with. Pushing her hurt and internal upheaval aside, she immersed her mind in her missing person case until exhaustion forced her to head home to her quiet, solitary apartment.

She heated a frozen dinner and ate by herself, spent another couple of hours making notes on the cases she'd brought home with her, then crawled between cold sheets that rasped against her sensitized skin as she tossed and turned in bed. Sleep was a long time coming, and this time when terrifying nightmares stole into her dreams and she woke in a cold sweat with tears on her cheeks, there was no one there to hold her and soothe her fears as before.

12

AFTER CHECKING IN with Brett at the office, Dean hung up the phone and scrubbed both hands down his face. His gut churned with dread. A possible buyout of Colter Traffic Control was happening faster than either of them had anticipated, and those important, life-altering decisions Dean had avoided thinking about now demanded his attention. An acceptance or refusal needed to be made within the next week, according to Brett and his attorneys handling the incoming offers and acquisition.

Believing Dean was out in some secluded mountain retreat without phone service, Brett hadn't expected him to call. Dean brought him up to date on his situation and how he'd been taken into custody and embroiled in a case of mistaken identity. They'd even had a good laugh over Dean believing Brett had sent Jo as his birthday surprise.

But things had quickly turned serious when Brett informed him of the latest bid from the company in San Francisco. As sorry as Brett and others were to cut short the first vacation Dean had taken in three years, they needed him back in the office as soon as possible to head up the meetings and make final decisions on the offer.

Over the past few days, any doubts he might have harbored about selling Colter Traffic Control had ebbed into absolute certainty. It was time for him to move on to something far more fulfilling than carrying on his father's legacy. He'd never asked for nor wanted the inheritance, but had taken over out of obligation to his father's memory, the people he'd employed, and in order to continue supporting his mother. He'd sacrificed his own wants and needs for others and had let fears overrule his relationship with Lora—though he now realized if she'd been that important to him he never would have allowed her to walk out of his life. He would have found a way to make a relationship, a marriage even, work, and to compromise and find a common ground that suited them both.

Now there was Jo to consider, who'd satisfied the restlessness in his soul and completed him in ways he never could have imagined. She was a woman he was more than willing to make sacrifices for and meet halfway in all things, to give and take equally—the kind of tradeoff his own father had never been willing to grant his own wife and family.

He wanted Jo to be a part of his future, yet he had no clear-cut idea where he fit into her life, if at all. While she'd given of herself physically to him, she'd withheld her emotions. Obviously, she harbored deep-rooted fears of her own, and whatever demons haunted her soul in the darkest hours of the night went a whole lot deeper than he'd originally thought or imagined.

"Damn," he muttered and flopped back on the hotel bed where he'd spent the last two nights—*alone*—and stared up at the ceiling. He wasn't ready to return to Seattle, not when he still had unfinished business with Jo, yet he knew he'd never shirk the responsibilities he still had waiting for him, obligations he'd made his own when he'd taken over his father's company. And that meant leaving Jo so he could be there to make final, important decisions.

He exhaled a harsh breath that did little to ease the frustration and tension gripping him. Staying away from Jo and keeping his distance for the past two days had been the hardest thing Dean had ever done, but he'd had no choice. She'd needed time to come to her own conclusions and figure out what she wanted from him.

He'd managed to keep himself busy sightseeing the city. Hell, he'd even had a good time with Noah that first night and enjoyed their easy comradery. And while her brother had openly asked if there was anything going on between him and his sister, Dean had skirted the issue—neither confirming or denying anything. Surprisingly, Noah had respected his evasion, yet Dean had no doubt that both brothers would hunt him down to serve up their brand of retribution if he ever hurt Jo.

He'd never deliberately cause Jo pain, yet it was nearly impossible to cultivate any kind of relationship with her when she'd detached herself from him. The obstinate woman knew where he was staying, had his number, and hadn't called—not even to say hello or see how he was doing. He'd graciously given her the space she seemed to need and time alone to think about all that had transpired between them and come around to his way of thinking. Now, with urgent matters waiting for him back home, he was forced to push the issue of *them*. There had to be some kind of compromise they could reach, unless she truly didn't want him in her life.

Remembering their last night together and all the emotion she'd poured into their lovemaking told him otherwise. She was running scared—of what, exactly, he hadn't yet pinpointed. But he was determined to chip away at those barriers and discover if they even had a chance together. And he had less than twenty-four hours to do so.

With that decision made, he drove his rental car over to Sommers Investigative Specialists. He greeted Melodie with a friendly smile that gained him entrance to Jo's office. He walked into the room after she answered his knock on the door with a soft, "Come in."

"Hey," she said in surprise as he approached her desk where she sat. "What brings you by?"

She was happy to see him—the delight shimmering to life in her eyes confirmed that she wasn't nearly as indifferent to him as she'd like him to believe. "You, of course," he said, and took up residence in the same spot he'd perched his hip two days earlier—right next to her seat.

She leaned back in her chair and absently toyed with the pen in her hand. "Done sightseeing already?"

He resisted the impulse to lift her from her chair, pull her into his embrace, and kiss her senseless, just to feel her soft and yielding in his arms again. But the truth beckoned, and there was no sense drawing out their inevitable conversation. "Jo...I'm leaving for Seattle tomorrow morning."

Her eyes widened, filling briefly with startled panic. That quick glimpse was all he needed to see to verify she was deliberately denying both of them time together that could possibly determine the fate of their future, and a relationship.

"I had a firm offer on the company," he went on, "and I need to be there for negotiations."

"So, you're going to sell the business?" Her voice sounded tight, but just as controlled as her emotions now seemed to be.

He nodded slowly. "If the price is right, yeah, I am."

She considered that for a long moment, her expression giving nothing away. "And then what are you going to do?"

A small smile touched his lips. "I don't know for certain, but the possibilities are endless." He grew serious. "When my father died I automatically stepped in to take over the business because it's what I believed was expected of me, but now I want to take the time to figure out what I want to do with the rest of my life instead of making a split-second decision based on everyone else's expectations. I can't deny that starting over is a scary prospect after relying on the security of my father's company for so long, but it's one of many challenges I'm more than ready to accept.''

"Starting over is never easy,'' she replied, her voice quiet, but filled with a depth and knowledge that caught his attention.

He tipped his head and made the spontaneous decision not to let her comment go by despite the emotional territory he might be boldly trampling upon. "Are you speaking from personal experience?''

She hesitated, her blue eyes darkening with subtle but unmistakable traces of regret. "Yeah, I guess I am.''

There were still so many things he needed to understand about Jo, and he was feeling desperate enough to push emotional issues that would finally give him insight to her deepest insecurities. And if after this conversation she still sent him away, he hoped he'd leave knowing the reasons why she couldn't give of herself.

"You know all about me, my past, and why I want to sell my father's company.'' And he knew of her devotion to her abduction cases. But one crucial piece of the puzzle that completed this woman was still missing, and he intended to fill in the gap. "Tell me, Jo, why did you quit the police force?'' he asked, his tone gentle, but firm.

Her lips tightened, and her eyes flashed with a defiance he'd grown used to. He wasn't at all surprised when she pushed back her chair, stood, and walked over to the windows overlooking the parking lot, putting more distance between them and automatically erecting emotional barriers.

One by one, he'd tear every last one down. "Was it because of what happened to Brian?" he persisted. All he knew was that her partner had been shot in the line of duty, but the details of that incident were what concerned him now. "Is that why you quit?"

Arms crossed tight over her chest, she turned around to face him again, seemingly struggling with whether or not to reveal such painful secrets. Long moments passed, and she finally said, "I quit the force because I was *responsible* for what happened to Brian." Her words were choked and as raw as the self-condemnation chasing across her features.

Despite believing he was prepared to hear anything, her brutal answer stunned him into absolute silence.

"*I'm* the reason why Brian is dead," she reiterated. A rush of tears filled her eyes, and she resolutely blinked them back.

"Tell me about it," he urged softly, aching for her and the obvious anguish swirling in the depths of her dark blue eyes.

She inhaled a shaky breath to gather her composure, and he waited patiently for her to make the decision to trust him. Finally, she did.

"When I went to work as a cop, because of my gender and slender size my colleagues constantly doubted my physical strength and endurance, and I had to work twice as hard at proving that I was capable of handling every aspect of my job.'' Frustration underscored her voice and she shook her head in disgust. ''But no matter how many two-hundred-pound men I managed to chase down and cuff, or the numerous times I had to restrain an obnoxious drunk or irate civilian, I never seemed to get the respect I deserved.

''Then I was paired up with Brian as a partner,'' she said, turning back to look out the window, her voice distant and far away, seemingly caught up in past memories. ''And for the first time since becoming a police officer I had the respect of a man and colleague. Brian believed in equality, and never once treated me as anything less than a fully trained cop. He never questioned my abilities, and he even gave me the confidence to believe in myself...and I repaid his faith in me by costing him his life.''

Dean watched a shudder course through her, and knew they'd just barely scratched the surface of all the pain and grief she'd kept locked away for too long. Standing, he closed the physical distance separating them, but kept his hands to himself. ''What happened, Jo?'' He needed to know everything.

She swallowed hard and met his gaze, her own glazed with a wealth of guilt. ''The two of us were on patrol, and we received a call to investigate a suspicious man who was hiding out in an abandoned house,'' she said, her voice hoarse. ''We went in and found the man in question, and he had a five-year-old boy with him. He had the boy's mouth taped shut and his hands tied behind his back, and it was obvious that he'd been kidnapped. Brian and I drew our revolvers and blocked the perp's exit from different doorways, but the other man had a gun, too. I told him to drop his weapon, and all he did was panic and thrust the kid away from him.

"We tried reasoning with the man, but he was so skittish and refused to cooperate. For the most part he kept his aim trained on me while we tried to talk him into giving up." She touched a hand to her chest and paused for a moment before continuing. "The adrenaline that flowed through my body was like nothing I've ever experienced before. My heart was pumping hard in my chest and my head was swimming with a thousand thoughts, but I managed to keep my gun steady. Then backup units arrived and he completely freaked out and threatened to shoot the little boy who was cowering and whimpering on the floor. And while I kept talking to the man to try and calm him, Brian eased his way closer to the kid, and that's when the perp lost it, redirected his aim, and shot Brian."

She visibly shuddered, as if reliving the awful moment. "Oh, God, Dean..." She looked at him, her tear-filled eyes reflecting deep pools of agony. "The second the goddamn perp shifted his gun to Brian, I should have fired my weapon without hesitation to stop him. I knew that, my mind screamed at me to pull the trigger, but everything happened so fast and all I could do was watch in horror as Brian took a bullet and crumpled to the ground."

She blinked, and a lone tear trickled down one cheek. Very gently, he wiped it away with the pad of his thumb, offering a small measure of comfort. Sensing she wasn't done, he remained quiet.

"The window behind the perp was busted out, and backup was there to watch what happened to Brian and they did what I couldn't do. They shot the guy and killed him before he could turn his weapon back on me." She swiped at another stray tear before he could do the deed himself—maintaining that in-control facade he knew to be a ruse. "All I can remember is dropping my gun and scrambling over to Brian. He'd been wearing a bullet-proof vest, but the bullet hit him in the neck and severed an artery and he was bleeding all over the place. I tried to put pressure on the wound and begged him not to die, but he drew his last breath in my arms." Her voice faded away on a note of despair.

You can't die. You can't. I won't let you. Dean's gut clenched as those words came back to haunt him—a hysterical plea straight out of the nightmare that had plagued Jo their first night together. Now her actions that evening made sense, and knowing the source of her pain, he pulled her into his embrace to console her.

Her body was tense and stiff, her arms still crossed protectively over her chest. Reluctantly, she accepted his brand of comfort, seemingly still struggling with the effort to remain tough and strong when at the moment she was as vulnerable and fragile as glass. His heart squeezed tight, and he wished he had the ability to make all those ugly, disturbing memories disappear.

But he didn't have that power, and so instead he opted for soothing words and gentle caressing sweeps of his hands down her unyielding back. "Jo...you couldn't have known that the guy was going to shoot Brian," he tried reasoning.

She lifted her head to meet his gaze, her expression filled with blame and self-reproach. "The moment that perp took his gun off of me to train it on Brian and threatened his life I should have pulled the trigger, no questions asked." She shook her head, her jaw clenching in bitterness. "I wasn't thinking straight, and not covering my partner went against everything I learned in training. Dammit, I couldn't follow through with pulling the trigger, and I proved to everyone from my brothers on down to my colleagues that when it came to making the kind of life or death decisions some cops face during their careers, I couldn't handle the job."

He resisted the urge to shake her, to make her realize that she couldn't wallow in blame and guilt forever. That she couldn't remain chained to the past or she'd never be able to embrace a full and emotionally satisfying future. "You made a mistake, Jo," he argued lightly. "It happens to the strongest of people sometimes."

She wriggled out of his arms and pushed him away, her mouth pinched with a frown. "That mistake cost a man his life, Dean," she said, angry now—at herself, possibly at him, and even fate for delivering such a devastating blow. "He was as close to a best friend as I've ever had. After the accident, I had no choice but to resign from the police force, for my sake and everyone else I worked with, all of whom didn't want a skittish partner. And I don't want to be responsible for another person like that ever again," she added in a raspy whisper.

Her emotional resistance was the crux of everything that led to them, he knew. She was afraid of making another *mistake*. Of letting anyone too close, caring too much, of trusting instincts she believed were no longer accurate or reliable. Afraid of experiencing more failure, more loss, more pain.

Unfortunately, life didn't come with any guarantees against heartache and misery.

"Does that include me?" His tone was soft, but his question was frank and ruthless, forcing her to face what she'd been avoiding for the past two days— *them.*

Her chin lifted a fraction and her gaze narrowed on him. "What, exactly, are you asking?"

He pushed his fingers into the front pockets of his jeans, trying to keep calm when his insides were twisting into a huge knot of turmoil. But he'd come this far with her and he wasn't about to leave without laying all his cards on the table, no matter what it might end up costing him personally.

"Are you allowing the incident with Brian to keep you from letting yourself trust in what's between us?" he asked. "What *can* be between us?"

She bristled defensively. "What's between you and

I has nothing to do with Brian or my past. We had a fling. An affair. Neither one of us made any promises to the other.''

Despite the desperation he heard in her voice, anger flared through him—that she'd reduced their relationship to something so superficial. "We might not have made any verbal promises," he agreed tightly, "but there was a hell of a lot more between us than just hot sex, and you know it, even if you won't admit it out loud." And if they weren't in a place where anyone could walk in on them, he'd push her up against the wall and prove it to her...make her melt with a kiss, make her moan with an intimate caress, and make her beg for what her body craved and her mind so obstinately refused to acknowledge. That she *needed* the physical and emotional connection they shared.

"I'm sorry," she whispered in an aching tone.

A muscle in his cheek flexed. He had no idea if she was apologizing for all that had happened between them, or if she was feeling contrite for what she couldn't bring herself to give to him. A commitment. And yes, promises, too. Either way, his annoyance and frustration mounted.

"I don't want your apology, Jo. I want *you*," he said, deciding that he was done catering to her fears when she held a huge part of his future in her hands. "And I'm optimistic enough to believe that we can find a way to make things work between us, even if it means long-distance commuting until I get things finalized with my father's company."

Her eyes widened in shock at his candid intentions, and she shook her head. "I'm not ready for that."

Would she *ever* be ready to take that leap of faith with him? he wondered. He stared at her as long seconds ticked past and came to realize that, for her, backing away from taking personal risks now equaled no chance of experiencing more pain. She was so wrapped up in the remorse of her past actions that she refused to move forward with her life. He planned to give her a forceful nudge. "Guilt is a powerful motivator, isn't it, Jo?"

Her cheeks flushed a warm shade of red. "I have no idea what you're talking about."

"Don't you?" he countered bluntly. "The guilt you feel over Brian's death motivates all your actions, whether you realize it or not. You lost Brian over a man who'd kidnapped a child, and now you pour all your extra time into finding abducted children. And you're always caught up in trying to be tough and in control and proving to everyone around you that you're strong and capable. You had a moment of weakness, Jo, and you have to get past the blame so you can forgive yourself and go on with your life." He softened his tone. "It's okay to be vulnerable, and it's more than okay to need someone. You can't let one incident rule the rest of your life."

She remained quiet, and he took advantage of her silence to further his argument. "I know this isn't something you want to hear, but I'm going to say it anyway. I'm falling in love with you, Jo." Harsh laughter escaped him. "Hell, who am I kidding? I'm already there."

Once the words were out in the open they felt right and undeniable and perfectly etched in his heart and soul. Closing the distance between them, he reached out and brushed his fingers along her silken cheek. "But maybe I need to wait for you to catch up and admit that you feel the same. Or maybe I'm a fool for believing you'll eventually come around and realize that you have nothing at all to prove to me. That I care about you and accept you just the way you are, mistakes and all."

Her eyes glittered with renewed moisture and conflicting emotions—longings, uncertainties, and deep-rooted fears. She chewed on her bottom lip, seemingly struggling with wanting to believe all he'd said, but allowing doubts to surface and shake her confidence.

She remained silent. Their gazes remained connected, but Dean's entire body felt hollow and empty, like he'd just lost an integral part of himself he never knew existed until he'd fallen in love with Jo. And that's exactly what had happened, when he'd least expected it, too.

Now there was nothing left to say to convince this stubborn woman standing in front of him that her fear of failure was a logical insecurity after all she'd been through, that she did have the ability to conquer her darkest fears if only she'd make the effort. Her emotional scars ran deep, wrapped up tight in guilt and regrets only she could absolve. And while he knew with certainty that she possessed the internal strength to banish all those demons that haunted her dreams, her soul even, she had to believe it for herself.

The door to Jo's office abruptly opened, and she visibly jumped and quickly swiped at the dampness clinging to her bottom lashes. She scowled at whoever had intruded into the room, and Dean glanced over his shoulder to find Cole standing in the middle of her office, a file folder in hand and a frown in place.

She shot her brother an annoyed look, which didn't do much to cover up the misery still reflected on her face. "When a door is closed, that usually means a person wants privacy, Cole."

Her brother's gaze took in how upset Jo was, then shifted to Dean. His stare turned harsh and penetrating, protective even. "I didn't know anyone was in here with you."

"Exactly," she said irritably. "Next time knock before you barge in."

Cole strolled up to the front of Jo's desk and tossed the file folder on top of other scattered papers, though his gaze never left Dean's. "Now that your name has been cleared, I thought you'd be long gone."

Didn't Cole wish, Dean thought. Refusing to let the other man intimidate him in any way, he shrugged. "Just tying up a few loose ends first," he replied easily, and let Cole come to his own conclusions about that comment.

The room grew silent for long seconds, then Cole spoke again. "Since you're here, it'll save Jo a phone call. I just received word from Vince. The guy who assumed your identity was taken into custody last night at a warehouse raid where undercover cops traced a stolen vehicle.''

A huge burden had been lifted off of Dean's shoulders, yet one still remained. One he knew he'd carry with him all the way back to Seattle. ''Thank you.'' Figuring it was time he broke the ice with Jo's brother, he extended his hand across the desk. ''That's the best news I've heard all day.''

Cole shook Dean's hand, the fierce lines creasing his expression easing a few degrees, but not completely. ''Looks like I owe you an apology for this entire misunderstanding,'' he said gruffly.

Dean managed a small smile. ''It's definitely been interesting.'' And the incident had changed his entire life.

Since Cole wasn't making any attempt to leave Jo's office before he did, Dean was forced to say his final goodbyes in front of her brother. He honestly didn't give a damn that Cole was watching his every move toward his sister. All Dean cared about was leaving Jo with the lasting impression that his feelings for her were genuine and real.

Cupping the back of her neck in his hand so she couldn't pull away, he kissed her trembling lips lightly, hoping like hell it wouldn't be the last time he was allowed the intimate privilege. Then he moved his mouth to her ear and murmured so only she could hear, ''When you're ready to let go of the past and embrace the future, you know where to find me.''

He exited her office, heard Cole follow behind, and before he could push through the front door, Cole stopped him.

"I have to ask," Cole said, his voice rough as he pushed his fingers through his hair in an agitated gesture. "What are your intentions toward Jo?"

Dean thought about Cole's brotherly question and realized Jo was the only person who could supply that particular answer. He shrugged. "That all depends on Jo's intentions toward *me.*"

And both he and Cole were better off letting Jo figure out what she truly desired all on her own, and in her own time.

13

"YOU CERTAINLY HAD yourself quite an adventurous trip to San Francisco."

Dean smiled across the restaurant table at his mother, Anne. It was his first night back in Seattle after leaving Jo, and while he'd spent a good part of the day in negotiation meetings at the office, he'd cleared his evening specifically to spend a few hours with his mother.

She'd asked about his shortened vacation, and during their main course he'd entertained her with how he'd been taken into custody by a feisty female bounty hunter in a case of mistaken identity. His mother had been at first shocked and appalled at the thought of him being arrested, then gradually found humor in the situation once he'd assured her that his name had been cleared. And while he'd mentioned Jo in the scheme of his story, for the time being he kept the intimate details of his relationship with her to himself.

"All things considered, it was one of the most enjoyable vacations I can ever remember taking," he replied, amusement still lingering in his voice. Done with his meal, he placed his fork on his plate and pushed the dish aside for the waiter to clear away. "Very spontaneous and fun, and just what I needed to clear my head."

"You do look more relaxed," Anne commented, then tipped her head and gently scrutinized his features. "But I have to admit I recognize that small, serious crease that appears between your brows when you have something important on your mind."

He chuckled at his mother's uncanny ability to read him and his shifting moods so well, a skill she'd developed when he was a kid and had spent too much time resenting the choices his father had made that didn't include him. "Actually, there are two things I need to talk to you about."

She leaned back in her chair as their server approached their table, took their dessert orders, and whisked away their dinner plates.

Once the waiter was gone, she asked, "Is everything okay?"

Drawing a deep, steady breath, he met her curious and concerned gaze. Despite being in her late fifties, his mother was still a beautiful woman and there seemed to be a new warmth and glow about her he'd never noticed before. Then again, had he ever really taken the time to notice the small changes and details around him since taking over the reins of his father's company?

The answer—no—jumped into his mind much too easily.

Since Jo, he seemed so in tune to subtle changes and even the mundane things he'd lived with and accepted for years...such as how quiet and empty his house was. How big his king-sized bed seemed for just one person. And how much he craved the kind of laughter and loving he'd experienced so briefly with Jo.

"Things are okay with me," he told his mother, knowing he lied. He wouldn't be completely whole until Jo came to her senses and realized they belonged together. "Except a few things happened on my trip to San Francisco and I've made some decisions that will affect you, too."

She folded her hands in her lap and waited patiently for him to continue.

He grinned wryly. "Would you believe I fell hard for the woman who took me into custody and dragged me all the way back to California?"

Her hazel eyes widened in surprise. "The female bounty hunter?"

He nodded, and refrained from correcting his mother with the politically correct term of "bail enforcement agent" that Jo insisted upon. "I know it happened quickly," he rushed on to explain, "but without a doubt I'm in love with her."

His mother's expression softened with genuine understanding, and without judgment. "There is no time limit on how long it takes a person to fall in love with someone, Dean. Sometimes those things happen when you least expect it." Leaning forward, she propped her elbows on the table and rested her chin on her laced fingers. "So why isn't she here with you so I can meet her for myself?"

Dean scrubbed a hand along his jaw, feeling familiar frustration build within him. He'd only been gone a day, yet he missed Jo like he'd never missed anyone in his life. "She's being more obstinate about admitting her feelings, but I'm hoping in time she'll eventually come around." While he was clinging to positive thoughts in terms of Jo meeting him halfway, he knew the agonizing possibility existed that she'd allow fears to ultimately rule her heart and emotions.

Anne smiled gently. "If this woman is what you truly want, I hope everything works out for you."

"Thanks, Mom." Her unconditional support meant a lot to him and made other momentous decisions easier to divulge. "For me, Jo's definitely 'the one.' The next step is up to her."

The waiter arrived, delivering two cups of steaming coffee with their slices of triple-layer chocolate cake. He poured cream into his coffee, then took a bite of the rich dessert which again reminded him of his time spent with Jo, but his mother held off on sampling her confection. Now it was her brows that creased and warned him she had something more serious to discuss.

"I know I've never said as much, but all I've ever wanted was for you to be happy, Dean," she said quietly.

His mother's words touched him deeply. "It's taken me a while to figure that out for myself, too, but I think I finally have a handle on what I want and need to do at this point in my life."

"Oh?" she asked, seemingly catching the underlying thread of foreshadowing in his tone.

He washed down a bite of the chocolate cake with a sip of coffee, and didn't mince words. "I've had an offer for the company, and I've decided to sell Colter Traffic Control."

Instead of the dread or fear he'd anticipated, her features expressed visible relief. "Will you think I'm an awful mother if I tell you that I'm glad?"

His brows rose. "Why would I think that?"

"Because I was hoping you'd sell the company from the day your father died," she said. "I always suspected that you took over the business out of obligation, but I think I always knew deep in my heart that given tangible choices, you wouldn't have chosen to carry on your father's legacy."

Dean's jaw nearly dropped at that revelation. "Why didn't you tell me how you felt?"

A small, apologetic shrug lifted her shoulders. "It's something you had to come to realize for yourself, and I didn't want you to resent *me* for making the suggestion of letting go of your father's business."

He shook his head, stunned. "I had no idea."

"I know." Emotion tightened her voice, and she reached across the table and squeezed his hand. "For all your father's faults, I do have to say you inherited his best qualities. You're extremely dedicated and you take your responsibilities seriously once you make up your mind to do something. Don't get me wrong. I'm proud of what you did, and I understand your reasons without even verbalizing them, but it's time for you to make your life what *you* want it to be.''

"And you? You'll be okay?" he asked, needing to hear from his mother that his decision wouldn't hurt her in any way or make her feel any less secure.

"I'm more than okay, Dean." She inhaled a slow breath before going on. "After living with your father for so many years and never really understanding his way of thinking, I just didn't know what it was that would make you content and satisfied, if that makes sense. When you took over the business after your father died, I thought you did it because that's what you wanted. Yet over the years I've seen you sacrifice so much to keep the company successful and thriving. Now, as a mother talking to her son, not to the single-minded businessman you've been, I'm so pleased to see you finally making your life and future a priority.''

He smiled. "Thanks, Mom.''

"And now, I have something to share with you, too.'' She toyed nervously with her fork, then revealed, "I've been seeing someone for the past few months.''

More surprises, but Dean supposed this evening was a night for revelations. "Why didn't you tell me?''

"You always seemed so busy and distracted, and I never imagined that things would turn so serious so quickly. Like you and your Jo, I've fallen in love with Ted, and I think it's time the two of you met.''

He grinned broadly. "Mom, I think that's wonderful, and I'd love to meet him."

"He treats me like a queen, dotes on me, and makes me feel so pampered and spoiled." She blushed like a young girl in the throes of a first crush. "I'm not used to that kind of attention, but I have to say I do like it."

Dean laughed, enjoying his mother's newfound happiness. "You deserve every bit of the attention, so enjoy it."

"Oh, I plan to." Her eyes sparkled with mischievous delight as she sipped her coffee. "So, tell me, what do you plan to do once you sell the company?"

Dean figured it would take a good four to six months to get all his personal business in order, and then he'd be free to strike out on his own, pursue interests, and start over. "I'm going to move to San Francisco."

"To be near Jo?" his mother guessed.

"Partly," he said, but knew he couldn't count on the relocation making any difference with Jo if she wasn't willing to commit herself to him and a relationship. "I really like the city and I know there are a ton of opportunities there, or wherever I might look. I just have to figure out which opportunity appeals the most."

"It seems you and I have finally learned to put ourselves first for a change, haven't we?"

"Yeah, we have." And it amazed him how one very special, stubborn, vulnerable woman could bring about such a huge, life-altering change for him.

Unfortunately, he faced the possibility of living the rest of his life without her.

JO TOSSED HER PENCIL onto her desk and exhaled a heavy sigh. If the past two days without Dean were filled with such deep, emotional misery, she didn't know how she was going to survive the rest of her life without him. She didn't feel like eating, she couldn't sleep at night, and her days were filled with distracting thoughts of him and their time together. She was even haunted by his final, parting words to her.

When you're ready to let go of the past and embrace the future, you know where to find me.

Such a simple statement, yet she found it so much easier to bury herself in her work and try to block out the pain of losing Dean. She knew she was in denial, shying away from grasping the courage to believe in everything he offered and represented: a man who loved her, despite her flaws and imperfect past. Using work as an excuse to avoid facing her deepest insecurities was not only ineffective, it was the coward's way out, she knew. And she abhorred that she lacked the internal fortitude to confront and reconcile her greatest weaknesses—which revolved around the inability to believe in herself, as well as forgive herself for the mistake that had ruled the past two years of her life.

Closing the file on the new case she'd been working on, she stood and went to the window in her office, trying to shake off her disheartened mood. Unfortunately the bright sunshine and clear view offered no escape from her disturbing thoughts or the more sensual memories of Dean—memories that had a way of edging into her mind when she least expected them.

"Jo, Roseanne Edwards is on line three for you." Melodie's voice drifted through the intercom on Jo's desk, snapping her out of her bout of regret. "She says it's an emergency."

"I'll take the call," she told Melodie, and moved back toward her desk.

Roseanne, a new client, had arrived first thing that morning and literally begged Jo to take on her abduction case. Yesterday her husband, Michael, had violated the terms of his bail for assault and battery to his wife, blatantly ignored restraining orders, and had kidnapped their eight-year-old daughter, Lily, when she'd gone outside to check the mail. According to Roseanne, she and Michael were embroiled in a nasty divorce case over his excessive drinking and abuse, and she'd expressed fear that her husband might hurt the young girl, since he had violent tendencies. While the police had been informed of the abduction, she'd contacted Jo to secure her services to help track her husband.

She picked up the receiver. "What's up, Roseanne?"

"He finally called," the other woman said, her tone high-pitched and near hysterical. "I heard Lily crying in the background and he's threatening to hurt her if I don't promise to cancel our divorce proceedings. I told him I'd do anything just so long as he lets her go, but he hung up on me and hasn't called back. Oh, God, what am I going to do?''

Jo tamped down the apprehension that tightened her own chest. "Roseanne, I'll do whatever I can to find your daughter, but you have to stay calm and focused for me.''

"I'll never forgive myself if he hurts Lily," she said, her voice catching on a sob.

"Nobody is going to hurt Lily, not if I can help it." It was a promise Jo had no right to give, but she was compelled to offer hope and assurance to Roseanne in any way she could. "I need some personal information from you about your husband to try and track him down quickly."

"I'll give you anything I have, just so long as you get my baby girl back."

It took Jo another five minutes to soothe the upset mother enough so that she could gather all the necessary account numbers, passwords, and authorization codes to run a trace on recent activity on their joint credit card accounts. The urgency of the case spurred her on, and once she hung up with Roseanne she jumped on the Internet and the phone to pull in long overdue favors from various sources. She contacted informants and even a retired detective her father used to be good friends with until she gained the valuable information she sought.

Within three hours she'd discovered that Michael Edwards had recently used one of those joint credit cards to check into a low-rate motel in Concord, approximately half an hour outside of Oakland. The trace was a prime piece of evidence, and just what Jo needed to track and find the man holding his own daughter hostage.

Gathering up her notes, she stuffed them into a file folder that also held Michael's picture, a faxed copy of the restraining order he'd violated, as well as all the necessary paperwork she needed to arrest the man for breaching the terms of his bond agreement. Just as she reached for her shoulder holster, Cole walked into her office and came to an abrupt stop when he saw her quick movements as she secured her revolver against her left side.

"Where are you off to?" he asked.

Jo clenched her jaw in annoyance. She didn't need an interrogation from her brother when time was of the essence, but she knew from experience that he'd never let her walk out the door without giving him an explanation. She kept it as succinct as possible. "I'm going to check a lead on the Edwards case."

Surprise transformed his taut features. "You know where Roseanne's husband is?"

Cole had been there that morning when Roseanne had sought Jo's services, and knew the details of the case. "Possibly," she replied, treading carefully with her answers. Slipping into her lightweight jean jacket, she adjusted the sides so it concealed her weapon and handcuffs. "I'll have a better answer for you once I verify the information I was given."

He scowled at her. "The man is said to be armed and dangerous, Jo. I'll have Noah go with you." He turned, stuck his head out the door, and before Jo could stop him he yelled down the hall, "Melodie, send Noah into Jo's office immediately."

Jo felt her temper rise and resisted the urge to pick up the brass paperweight on her desk and pitch it at her brother's thick head. "I don't need or want a baby-sitter, Cole. I can handle this case on my own." Her tone was adamant, her words succinct.

He didn't seem to notice. "I'm not giving you a choice," he refuted. "You either take Noah with you, or I take over the case."

His ultimatum struck her like a physical blow and once again made her all too aware that her brother didn't trust her to handle things on her own.

Noah entered the room on the tail end of Cole's comment, took in the standoff and tension between brother and sister, and frowned. "What's going on?"

Cole waved a hand toward Jo, his expression creased with annoyance. "Jo's following a dangerous lead and she's going to get herself hurt, or worse."

Her cheeks heated with indignation, and she rounded her desk to close the distance between her and her brothers, feeling the onslaught of a long-overdue battle brewing deep within.

"I'm going to tell you both *exactly* what's going on," she said, reaching deep inside for the kind of strength and fortitude she hadn't allowed herself to grasp for too long. "I'm tired of being coddled and treated like I don't know the business or what the hell I'm doing." She pinned Cole with a direct look. "I just went through all this doubt and upheaval from you with Dean when I wanted you to trust in my instincts. Dean was and is an innocent man, and I was right. Yet here we are having this same conversation, with you questioning what I'm capable of, what I can handle, and if I'll make the right decisions.'' Her voice cracked, and she realized that she was just as much at fault for *letting* them overwhelm her with their take-charge personalities. Not anymore. "I've had enough of your overbearing, dominating attitudes.''

Cole looked stunned by her outburst, obviously having no clue how she'd felt, while Noah regarded her with equal measures of surprise and amusement. Neither said a word, and she took advantage of the silence.

"I love you guys,'' she said, meaning the heartfelt declaration. "You've done so much for me and you've always been there when I needed you the most. When Mom died you took care of me, and when Dad passed away you both did your best to raise me. But you've also taken that responsibility to the extreme, beyond where it all should have ended when I graduated from college and decided to become a cop.''

"And look at what happened,'' Cole said gruffly, referring to Brian's death.

His reference hurt, but she pushed the sting aside, refusing to let anything deter her from this overdue discussion. "How long do you intend to remind me of the mistake I made? I know I screwed up, but I can't dwell on the past forever. I have to trust in myself and my instincts again and I can't do that if the two of you are constantly trying to shelter me from harm.''

"We just don't want you to get hurt," Noah tried to explain.

"And I understand that. I really do." She swallowed the tight knot in her throat so she could finish. "I might not have given either of you much reason to believe in me because of what happened in the past, but there are some things I have to do for myself. And while I'd really appreciate your support, if you can't accept my decisions or trust in my abilities, I can go to work for another agency who will. The choice is yours."

Cole wasn't at all pleased that she'd managed to turn the ultimatum back to him, yet there was a glimmer of pride in the depth of his eyes that gave Jo hope. "We don't want you going anywhere else," he said, his tone sincere.

Relief rushed through her, yet she didn't let her victory show. "Then we start compromising." Which was the basis of any good, solid relationship, she thought, drawing on the advice that a smart older woman had offered her and Dean. "I'll be extra careful when I'm out in the field, and you stop doubting what I'm trained to do and quit smothering me."

"Fair enough," Noah said, answering for the two of them.

"Then we have a deal." She smiled for the first time in days, and grabbed her folder of information off her desk. "And now, I'm off to check out my lead…on my own."

This time, no one stopped her, and it was such a liberating feeling to walk out the door without an argument hanging over her head or her brothers' words filling her with doubts and insecurities. Now she had a case to concentrate on, and a little girl to bring home to her worried mother.

She made the drive to Concord in twenty-four minutes, pulled into the shabby motel parking lot where Roseanne's husband had last made a credit card transaction, and brought her vehicle to a stop in front of the registration office. She entered the building and explained to the young clerk behind the desk the urgency of her situation and that she needed Michael Edwards's room number. He resisted at first, citing motel policies, but was ultimately swayed to release the information when she'd let him glimpse her holster and weapon and gave a quick flash of her P.I. badge.

Michael's room was on the second floor, and Jo silently approached the door and listened for sounds or voices. She heard a man's rough voice shouting, his words slightly slurred, followed by a loud thump, and a little girl's painful scream.

A chill slithered through Jo and her heart pumped furiously in her chest. She had to reach Lily, knew the young girl's life was in danger, but Jo also realized that even if she could get Michael to open the door he most likely would keep the safety chain secured so she couldn't get inside. And she wouldn't risk antagonizing the violent man and possibly have him take his anger out on his daughter any more than he already had.

Frustration and fury swirled within her, and she returned to her vehicle to call for police backup from her cell phone. She was assured that a squad car would be there within fifteen minutes. To Jo, that seemed like an eternity when a little girl's life was at stake.

Just as she disconnected the line with a muttered curse, a small compact car zipped through the parking lot and came to a stop right below Michael's room. The neon sign on the roof of the car indicated pizza delivery, and since the parking lot was near empty of guest vehicles she hoped and prayed that Michael Edwards was the one who'd had a hankering for an Italian meal.

She wasted no time pocketing her Mace and grabbing a wad of cash from her purse, then hopped out of the Suburban and stopped the delivery person as he started up the concrete steps. He was so startled by her sudden appearance that when she asked what room he was making the delivery to, he gave her the number, which matched Michael's.

"I need to deliver that pizza," she told the teenager.

A skeptical look pinched his features and he shook his head. "I can't let you do that."

She didn't have time to cajole his cooperation, so she opted for the hard-line approach. "Look, I'm a cop and the man in the room is not only on the run from the law, but he's prone to violence. Trust me when I say I'm doing you a huge favor by delivering this pizza for you.'' Fear lit his pale blue eyes, and she took advantage of his apprehension and retrieved the cardboard box from his grasp, then shoved the bills into his hand. "There's enough to cover the cost of the pizza, plus a huge tip for you.''

He took one look at the money in his hand and decided not to argue further, seemingly figuring he was getting the better end of the deal. He jumped back into his car and hightailed it out of the parking lot and onto the main road.

Not wanting to spare another second, Jo took the stairs two at a time, knocked on Michael's door and announced, "Pizza delivery.''

She heard low muffled sounds and words she couldn't make out, then seconds later locks unbolted and the safety chain slid free from the latch. The door opened a few inches, revealing a burly, unkempt man dressed in boxer shorts and a stained T-shirt. His hair was long and oily from not being washed, and the stench of body order and liquor that slipped up her nostrils nearly made her gag.

Still blocking the door and not allowing her to see inside, he handed her a ten-dollar bill.

She didn't take the cash. "Umm, the total came to eleven seventy-six,'' she said, hoping he'd move away to get more money and give her the space she needed to maneuver herself inside.

"Goddamn expensive pizza,'' he grumbled and

took two steps to the left to grab something off the nightstand—his wallet.

He fumbled through the bills and she nudged the door open wider to peer beyond the bed dominating the room. Her stomach turned over when she saw the little girl curled up in the corner, her eyes wide with terror and a bruise on her cheek. Her arms were secured behind her back and Michael had taped her mouth shut to keep her quiet. The whole scene was too reminiscent of another time, another place, and Jo's entire body flashed hot, then cold.

Dammit, where were the cops?

She'd come this far and wasn't willing to give up the leverage she'd gained. She focused on the one thought filling her mind, which was saving the little girl. Daringly, she stepped inside the room with the pizza box still in her hands, but Michael blocked her path before she could go any farther.

"What the hell are you doing?" he demanded, his face flushing red with the beginning signs of rage.

She looked up at the solidly built man in front of her, and despite the sudden anxiety gripping her she forced a sweet smile. "I'm delivering your pizza, and a little something extra." Calling on strengths she never even knew she possessed, along with her martial arts training, she planted her foot into his belly and shoved him hard. The breath whooshed out of him and the force of her kick sent him stumbling back into the room, which also gained her full entrance. Tossing the cardboard box onto the bed, she withdrew her can of Mace and aimed it straight at his face.

"Don't move, Michael," she ordered. "You're under arrest."

He laughed menacingly, unthreatened by her choice of weapon. Still trying to gulp air into his lungs, he staggered toward a small table. Seeing the revolver resting there that he was after, Jo automatically dropped her Mace and withdrew her gun at the same time he picked up his and pointed it straight at her.

Adrenaline rushed through her blood. She started to sweat and her whole body trembled as old memories washed over her. She blocked the awful recollections the best she could and amazingly enough managed to keep her revolver leveled on Michael's chest.

She chanted the words Dean had left her with and she now drew strength from, *believe in herself. Believe, believe, believe.*

Her finger curled around the trigger. "Drop your gun," she told him, hating the slight quiver that found its way into her voice.

He gripped his pistol tighter, though his aim wasn't at all steady. "My wife has taken everything away from me, and I've got nothing left to lose." A malicious smile curved the corners of his mouth. "So, you shoot me and I kill the girl."

Believe, believe, believe, Jo's mind screamed, knowing the test she was about to face. A test she'd failed before. Before he could fully train his gun on the little girl in the corner, Jo fired off the first shot, the blast of sound deafening in the small room.

Her bullet hit Michael in the right shoulder, knocking him on his backside from the impact. He hit the ground with a hard thud, and the gun in his hand flew across the carpeted floor. She kicked the weapon aside, far out of reach, and unclasped her handcuffs from her holster to restrain him.

Wounded and in pain, Michael didn't have much strength to struggle, and she manacled his wrists and left him lying on his stomach. She hadn't killed him, but she'd saved Lily's life, and that's all that mattered to Jo. She'd leave Michael's fate up to the authorities.

She moved to the little girl and unbound her hands and untaped her mouth. Lily let out a sob and hurled herself into Jo's embrace, wrapping her arms tight around her neck and clinging with all her might. She held the frightened girl and rocked and soothed her with comforting words, her own emotions just as raw.

She'd believed. And she'd proved to herself, no one else, that she had the internal strength and ability to make right choices and follow through.

She'd fought the good fight here, and now she was ready to confront another fear. Life was too damn short and too uncertain, and she wasn't about to give up the one person who'd given her every reason to believe in herself.

14

AFTER A DELAYED FLIGHT to Seattle, she finally brought her rental car to a stop at the curb in front of Dean's house late Friday night, trying to calm the sudden nervous flutters taking flight in her belly. She'd had plenty of time to give herself a pep talk and prepare for this moment of reckoning. While she felt confident of her own personal decision, she had no idea what to expect from Dean with her impromptu visit—a warm welcome, or a cool reception?

Ultimately, his initial reaction didn't matter, because she wanted Dean, and she was willing to fight for him. For them.

Exiting the small compact, she made her way up to the door. A light shone through the front window, and she hoped that he was home, though the possibility existed that he'd be out celebrating his birthday. And if that was the case, she'd camp out in the car until he arrived home, because she intended to be his birthday present. Luckily, he answered on her first knock, looking completely surprised to see her.

"Jo," he said, his gaze taking in her presence as if he couldn't believe it was really her.

He looked so damned sexy and appealing in nothing but his pair of soft cotton sweatpants that it took all her effort to refrain from throwing herself into his arms and letting his solid warmth envelop her. She'd missed that special connection they shared. She'd missed *him.*

She summoned a bright, hopeful smile. "Happy birthday."

His dark brows lifted skeptically. "You came all the way to Seattle to wish me a happy birthday?"

She nodded, unable to blame him for being cautious about her sudden appearance when she'd given him no reason to believe that she'd come around. Especially after the way she'd rejected his love. However, after everything she'd been through in the past few days, she refused to let any uncertainties get the best of her.

"And I'm here to give you a birthday present that can only be appreciated in person." When he said nothing else, just stared at her with those searching green eyes, she swallowed the tight knot in her throat and asked, "Can I come in?"

"Uh, yeah, sure." He stepped back, waving her inside as if she was an old acquaintance stopping by for a casual chat, not the lover she'd recently been. "I was just having a slice of the strawberry pie my mother brought over for my birthday. Care for a piece?"

She followed him into the kitchen and spied the half-eaten dessert at the dining table. "No, thank you."

He slid back into his chair, picked up his fork, and

resumed eating the pie, a small smile teasing the corner of his mouth. "I bet if they were chocolate-covered strawberries you wouldn't have refused."

She was encouraged by the fact that he was flirting with her, despite being as distant to her now as she'd been with him days ago. "You're probably right."

She stood across the small room, unable to gauge his mood, or even where she stood with him anymore. He wasn't making her visit easy, but then he had no idea why she was there or what she wanted.

Leaning against the low counter behind her and bracing her hands on the edge, she inhaled a deep breath. "Dean, there's something I need to tell you."

"Okay." Finished with his dessert, he set his fork on his plate and pushed the dish aside. Reclining in the chair and crossing his arms over his bare chest, he gave her his undivided attention.

She then proceeded to tell him about Michael Edwards, the daughter he'd kidnapped, and how she'd found the courage and fortitude to not only draw her weapon, but pull the trigger to save Lily's life—without second-guessing herself.

A tremulous smile curved her lips. "And the best thing is, I walked away from the situation with absolutely no regrets."

"I know, and I was so damn proud of you for what you did," he said softly and with a wealth of satisfaction shining in his eyes. "And I got the impression that your brothers are proud of you, too."

Both Cole and Noah had been extremely supportive and, yes, proud of what she'd done. Then it dawned on her that Dean was already aware of her accomplishment. "You knew all this?" she asked incredulously. "How?"

His shoulders rolled in a lazy shrug. "Noah called to tell me what happened, thinking I'd want to come back to Oakland and be there for you."

Her chest tightened, and she stated the obvious. "But you didn't come back."

"No, I didn't." He stood and closed the space separating them. "But for one very good reason."

"And what reason is that?" she asked, her voice hoarse.

"This time, *you* had to be the one to come to *me*," he said, caressing the tips of his fingers along her cheek, his touch like a healing balm to her soul. "And I knew you couldn't do that until you were ready to admit that we had a future together."

Her entire body shuddered with relief, but her fingers remained clutched around the edge of the counter behind her. "I'm here now." Her simple words said it all.

He smiled gently, his eyes turning a warm, patient hue of green. "So you are."

He wanted more, and she gave him everything she had, all the honesty in her heart, knowing she had nothing left to lose. "I'm not completely over my fears and insecurities, but I can deal with anything so long as you're by my side. You're the reason I found the courage to believe in myself and pull that trigger."

"I had nothing to do with it, sweetheart," he refuted, seemingly not wanting to take any credit. "I always knew you possessed the strength to trust in your own instincts. I'm just glad it didn't take you long to figure it out for yourself."

She licked her dry lips, and willed her racing heart to calm. "And right now, those same instincts are telling me that I can't live without you."

He tipped his head, his gaze locking on hers. "Are they telling you anything else?"

"Yeah, they are." Need and longing swelled within her, and she didn't hesitate to embrace the feeling, or share it with this incredible man who'd changed her life for the better. "I love you, Dean Colter. And I'm not about to compound my mistakes by letting you go."

He framed her face in his big hands and smiled at her with the kind of deep, abiding emotions that knew no bounds. "That's exactly what I wanted to hear, Joelle Sommers."

Lowering his head, he sealed their lips, kissing her deeply, thoroughly, hungrily, until she melted in his arms and let him have his way with her mouth.

"So, what are we going to do about us?" he asked in between soft, lingering kisses along her lips, her jaw.

She threaded her fingers through the silky hair at the nape of his neck, reveling in the texture and warmth. "That all depends on you and where you want to live," she said, her tone breathless. "I'll follow you anywhere."

"Do you have any objections to me following you right back to Oakland?" he murmured.

His hot breath fanned against her skin, making her shiver and arousing her from head to toe. "You would do that?"

"Oh, absolutely. Just try and keep me away," he growled against her neck, then skimmed his lips up toward her ear and nibbled on her lobe. "I can commute until the sale of the business is finalized, but once that's done, I'm all yours."

Happiness bloomed like a new and fresh start for her. "Oh, I do like the sound of that."

He pulled back, and while his hands remained tangled in her hair, his gaze sought hers. "What about your brothers? Everything okay there?"

She nodded. "We've come to an understanding about me, my abduction cases, and what I can handle. A compromise if you will," she said with a sassy grin. "I think my brothers know exactly where I stand, and if they don't, I have no problem telling them."

He chuckled. "That's my girl. By the way, where are you hiding my birthday present?"

"Under my clothes."

He waggled his brows provocatively as his hands slid down her back and over her bottom. "Do I get to unwrap you?"

"Not this time." She moved out of his embrace and gently pushed him back toward his chair until he was once again sitting in the wooden seat. Then she took a few steps back to give him the best possible view of her presentation. "I believe I owe you a strip-tease for your birthday, the one you were expecting when I first took you into custody." She began unbuttoning her blouse and winked at him.

The flare of heat that ignited in the depth of his eyes told her that he appreciated her thoughtful gift. "How do you feel about getting married?" he asked.

She parted the cotton material and let it slowly slide down her arms to the floor. "How do you feel about having a bounty hunter as a wife?" she countered as she unclasped her lacy bra, and strategically removed it with one arm still covering her breasts.

"I'm not crazy about the idea," he admitted, frowning since she wasn't letting him see her naked just yet, "but I'm thinking we can find a way to compromise. How do you feel about having a partner on your road trips?"

"I'd like that." Kicking off her sandals, she turned around so that he was looking at her bare back, unbuttoned and unzipped her jeans, then slowly inched them down while giving her hips an enticing shimmy for effect. She glanced coyly over her shoulder at him, found him staring at her bottom, and smiled at his body's blatant reaction to her drawn-out strip. "At least until we start having a family of our own."

His surprised gaze leapt back up to hers. "You want that?"

She pushed the denim all the way down her legs and kicked them off. Then she turned around to face him, wearing a pair of lacy white panties, with her palms cupping the fullness of her breasts. "I would *love* that with you."

Her heart pounded at the wondrous look in his eyes, the complete and utter fulfillment...which ebbed into a desire and need that made every pulse-point in her body throb with equal intensity.

"Let me see, Jo," he said huskily.

She turned around again and hooked her thumbs into the waistband of her panties. "This is the 'tease' part of the strip." The scrap of material skimmed down and off. She tossed the piece of lingerie over her shoulder and it landed in his lap, right on top of his huge erection. "Bull's-eye."

He managed a strangled laugh. Picking up her undies, he rubbed them against his cheek, inhaled her scent, and groaned. "You already know that you'll get yours later."

"That's what I'm hoping," she said impudently, and finally gave him the full frontal view he'd been waiting for.

His eyes grew hot as he visually consumed her, his breathing labored. She felt incredibly feminine and desirable as she glided toward him, and bent low to draw his sweatpants down and off, then toss them aside. Kneeling in front of his spread thighs, she wrapped her fingers around the rigid length of his penis and brought him to the very brink with the stroke of her hand, the heat of her mouth, and the sensual swirls of her tongue—until he begged her to stop and urged her back up.

She moved over him, straddling his thighs as he

gripped her hips. He guided her down, and she was so ready for him that he slid all the way into her, deep and hard, tight and wet, a perfect, luxurious fit that made them both moan in unison.

His hands spread over the slope of her back to press their bodies intimately closer, and she brought his lips to hers and whispered, "Happy birthday, Dean," then rocked her hips rhythmically against his and sent them both over the edge and straight into bliss.

Once they regained their breath, Dean lifted his head from her neck and smiled wickedly at her, something Jo knew she'd never get tired of seeing on a daily basis.

"You're the one guilty of theft, you know," he drawled playfully. "And you do realize, don't you, that I'm going to have to take *you* into custody this time."

She managed a grin of her own. "Whatever for?"

He kissed her lips, softly, gently. "For stealing my heart. And your sentence is going to be life...as my wife."

It was time Jo was more than willing to serve.

* * * * *

Watch for Cole and Melodie's story in
A SHAMELESS SEDUCTION
Harlequin Temptation Heat
Summer 2002

USA Today Bestselling Author

NAN RYAN

The Scandalous Miss Howard

The boy who left to fight in the
Confederate army twenty years ago
had been a fool. He had trusted the
girl who promised to wait for him.
He had trusted the friend who
betrayed him. Now he has come home
to Alabama to avenge the loss of what they
stole from him—his heart, his soul, his world.

Laurette Howard, too, lost her innocence with the
news that the boy she loved had died in the war, and
with the loveless marriage that followed. Then
Sutton Vane arrived in Mobile, releasing the sensual
woman that had been locked away. She surrendered
to a passion so scandalous, it could only be destiny.
But was it a passion calculated to destroy her...
or to deliver the sweet promise of a love that
refused to die?

**"Nan Ryan knows how to
heat up the pages."
—Romantic Times**

MIRA®

MNR893

Back by popular request…
those amazing Buckhorn Brothers!

Once and Again

Containing two full-length novels by
the Queen of Sizzle,

USA Today bestselling author

LORI FOSTER

They're all gorgeous, all sexy and all single…at least for now!
This special volume brings you the sassy and seductive
stories of Sawyer and Morgan Buckhorn—offering you
hours of *hot, hot* reading!

Available in June 2002 wherever books are sold.

And in September 2002 look for FOREVER AND ALWAYS,
containing the stories of Gabe and Jordan Buckhorn!

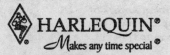
HARLEQUIN®
Makes any time special ®

HARLEQUIN
Temptation.

It's hot...and it's out of control!

This spring, the forecast is hot and steamy!
Don't miss these bold, provocative, ultra-sexy books!

PRIVATE INVESTIGATIONS by Tori Carrington
April 2002
Secretary-turned-P.I. Ripley Logan never thought her first job
would have her running for her life—or crawling into
a stranger's bed....

ONE HOT NUMBER by Sandy Steen
May 2002
Accountant Samantha Collins may be good with numbers, but
she needs some work with men...until she meets sexy but
broke rancher Ryder Wells. Then she decides to make him a
deal—her brains for his bed. Sam's getting the better of the
deal, but hey, who's counting?

WHAT'S YOUR PLEASURE? by Julie Elizabeth Leto
June 2002
Mystery writer Devon Michaels is in a bind. Her publisher has
promised her a lucrative contract, *if* she makes the jump to
erotic thrillers. The problem: Devon can't write a love scene to
save her life. Luckily for her, Detective Jake Tanner is an
expert at "hands-on" training....

Don't miss this thrilling threesome!

HARLEQUIN®
Makes any time special ®

HARLEQUIN
Temptation

THE WRONG BED

What happens when a girl finds herself in the *wrong* bed...with the *right* guy?

Find out in:

#866 NAUGHTY BY NATURE by Jule McBride
February 2002

#870 SOMETHING WILD by Toni Blake
March 2002

#874 CARRIED AWAY by Donna Kauffman
April 2002

#878 HER PERFECT STRANGER by Jill Shalvis
May 2002

#882 BARELY MISTAKEN by Jennifer LaBrecque
June 2002

#886 TWO TO TANGLE by Leslie Kelly
July 2002

Midnight mix-ups have never been so much fun!

HARLEQUIN®
Makes any time special ®

Visit us at www.eHarlequin.com

HTNBN2

What is your secret fantasy?

Is it to have your own love slave, to be seduced by a stranger, or to experience total sexual freedom?
Enjoy all of these and more in Blaze's newest miniseries

Heat up your nights with...

#17 EROTIC INVITATION by Carly Phillips
Available December 2001

#21 ACTING ON IMPULSE by Vicki Lewis Thompson
Available January 2002

#25 ENSLAVED by Susan Kearney
Available February 2002

#29 JUST WATCH ME... by Julie Elizabeth Leto
Available March 2002

#33 A WICKED SEDUCTION by Janelle Denison
Available April 2002

#37 A STRANGER'S TOUCH by Tori Carrington
Available May 2002

Midnight Fantasies—The nights aren't just for sleeping...

Makes any time special ®

Visit us at www.eHarlequin.com

HBMF